THE SEVENTH CIRCLE

OTHER WORKS BY BENET DAVETIAN

The Montreal Experience
Reprieve in Sarajevo
The Essene Gospel of Peace
(audio version)

THE
SEVENTH
CIRCLE

Benet Davetian

RONSDALE

1996

THE SEVENTH CIRCLE
Copyright © 1996 Benet Davetian

RONSDALE PRESS
3350 West 21st Avenue
Vancouver, B.C., Canada
V6S 1G7

Set in Bembo 12pt on 14½
Typesetting: The Typeworks, Vancouver, B.C.
Printing: Hignell Printing, Winnipeg, Manitoba
Cover Design: Ewa Pluciennik

The paper used in this book is Miami Vellum. It is recycled stock containing no dioxins. It is totally chlorine-free (TCF) as well as acid-free (therefore of archival quality). The paper is made from at least 10% post-consumer waste.

The publisher wishes to thank the Canada Council and the British Columbia Cultural Services Branch for their financial assistance.

Canadian Cataloguing in Publication Data

Davetian, Benet, 1947-
The seventh circle

ISBN 0-921870-38-8

I. Title.
PS8557.A624S48   1996   C813'.54   C95-911220-0
PR9199.3.D38S48   1996

Acknowledgements

The author would like to thank the publishers of Ronsdale Press, Ronald and Veronica Hatch, for their extraordinarily patient and enriching editorial direction; Patricia Johnston for her tireless feedback, copy-reading and friendship; writers Henry Beissel, Neil Bissoondath, Michel Choquette, Linda Ghan, and P. Scott Lawrence and sociologists H. Taylor Buckner, Pearl Crichton, and John P. Drysdale for their creative and moral support.

A slightly different version of "The Forbidden Zone" was published by the *Alaska Quarterly Review,* Spring: 1995.

With the exception of *Ten and a Half Ounces Per Day* and *In Transit*, which contain biographical as well as fictional passages, the stories in this book are fictional and any resemblance to individuals living or dead is only coincidental.

For
my family and my friends,
who continued to offer love and support
even though the writing of this book
required long stretches of solitude.

So, if you can escape these lands of darkness
and see the lovely stars on your return,
when you repeat… "I was there,"
be sure that you remember us to men.

THE SEVENTH CIRCLE, HELL
Canto XVI
Dante, *The Divine Comedy*

Contents

Preface

The stories in this book developed from a series of journeys that I undertook over a number of years. Some have asked if the stories really happened, if I observed them. The answer to this question is always difficult for a writer of fiction. He may have seen a story unfold, but it is only through the writing of the story that he gets to meet "the man within the man" and "the woman within the woman" of his characters. Certainly the backgrounds to these stories are historically accurate; the incidents described are documented; I have not tampered with fact. But it has been necessary for me to employ the writer's imagination—or perhaps even suspend it during certain moments—so that the characters themselves may feel free to tell their stories as *they* have understood them. Perhaps only in this way does brute facticity become intelligible and take on a human face. It would be better to say, then, that I have purposefully merged the real with the fictional. Indeed that may be the only fair way to tell stories such as these.

Benet Davetian
Montreal, 7 February 1996

Pilgrimage

Ibrahim is one of the oldest names, shared without argument or complaint by Arabs, Jews, and Christians. Ibrahim and Abraham are the same and mean "He who is blessed with the grace of God."

In very ancient times, Ibrahim, or Abraham, was a holy name chosen for sons of whom great things were expected. Today it is a common name, given to rich and poor alike, to those who worship as well as those who prefer to leave the heavens alone.

Mohammed knew that if ever he had a son he would call him Ibrahim. He had always liked the name. It signified strength and honour for him.

Mohammed thought often of this yet unborn son. It was difficult to work the farm alone. His own father had died young and he had been left with the land when he was barely a man. His good neighbours had rallied to his side and helped him during the harvests. But it embarrassed him to accept their help. He had been raised to believe that a man was not altogether a man until he had fathered a son to work alongside him. Even though he loved and cherished his daughter, he wanted a son now. He needed a son now.

His wife Khadijeh felt his distress and wished very much to be pregnant with a boy. She too loved her daughter and was proud of her. But like most women in her culture who hadn't yet mothered a son with strong arms to plant a field and swift legs to run after a herd, Khadijeh felt that she had yet to fulfil her marriage vows.

One day in the spring of Mohammed's twenty-eighth year, Khadijeh told him that she was pregnant. "Allah willing, it will be a son," she said. Mohammed's heart soared and a light streamed into his eyes. He put his arms around his wife and felt very grateful.

Khadijeh went to sleep that night certain that her prayers had been answered. She was sure that the child would be a boy. But Mohammed was unable to sleep. Would it be a son or a daughter? And how to wait the long months to find out? Sleepless with excitement and uncertainty, he left the house and hurried to the low hill which rose behind the farm. He knelt in the sandy grass at the foot of the hill, raised his arms, and pleaded with Allah that the child be a son.

With the first light of dawn, Mohammed went outside the house and used a stick to make marks in the sand—one for each of the years he had lived and one for each of the years needed for a boy to become strong enough to work a farm. Then he carefully added up all the marks. There were forty-five of them. He reckoned that he would be forty-five by the time his son would be old enough to manage the farm—the family would be safe if he were suddenly taken too ill to work. Tilling the hard earth and caring for the small herd under the burning sun of that land aged a man quickly.

Sometimes during his daily prayers his mind would wander and he would dream what a great thing it would be if he could one day produce a little more food than they needed to survive. Perhaps he and his son could then make the pilgrimage to the holy city of Mecca. Neither he nor his father had ever been able to afford the journey. The pilgrimage to Mecca meant much to Mohammed.

*

Mohammed's prayers were answered. Khadijeh gave birth to a boy in the very same house where Mohammed himself had been born. And the child was delivered by the same midwife who had delivered him twenty-nine years ago.

Mohammed looked at the frail infant and his face lit up with joy. For a moment he felt certain that Allah was on his side. He turned to the midwife and said, "Allah has sent his angels to this house and you have helped open the door for them. I am grateful to you."

The aged midwife put her hand to her lips and touched her forehead in a gesture of reverence. "Allah Akbar," she said. And then she put her hand to her lips again and touched Mohammed's forehead, blessing him just as she had done the day she delivered him into the world.

Mohammed looked at the infant tenderly and said, "His name will be Ibrahim." And with that, he went out of the house and hurried to the hill where he had prayed for a son. He walked with the quick long steps of a confident man. He fell on his knees at the foot of the hill and thanked his God. He felt the happiness of a man who is suddenly taken out of grave danger and told that all will be well. He clutched handfuls of the sandy earth and threw them up in the air, shouting, "Allah Akbar, Allah Akbar," over and over again.

He hadn't felt this young and happy since he had been a boy, swimming without a care in the river that kept his village green. The river had shrunk since and become narrow and shallow. But what did it matter, he thought. Ibrahim was born now. Ibrahim would be his fertile valley.

*

Mohammed's village lay seventeen kilometres northwest of the city of Baidoa. He had lived in the village all his life. As was the custom in Somalia, a man who didn't migrate to one of the large towns to seek his fortune did better to stay close to his own village. It wasn't easy for someone from one clan to gain acceptance in another; it had been so during hundreds of years of tribal quarrel and mistrust.

There were six large clans in Somalia and a host of subclans. People knew their entire family, including cousins twice removed. It was important for people to know their roots if they were to tell friends and enemies apart. So entire genealogies were kept in memory and transmitted from generation to generation.

This nation of multiple lineages was hardly the place for glib talk of unity and common purpose. Yet with the coming of the foreigners many years ago, a central government had been imposed on this land where each clan considered itself its own best governor. And when the foreigners had left some time later, a dictator had appeared to fill the vacuum of power and he had forced the leaders of the clans to link arms and pay him homage. The clans had felt coerced and humiliated by this false unity. They had sworn that they would one day have their revenge.

Mohammed's village consisted of sixty-four people. They were Mohammed's kinship group or *rer*. They claimed a common descent from an ancestor who had moved there five hundred years ago. The ancestor had been one of the great herdsmen who roamed the rich virgin pastures before anyone came from any foreign nation to measure and survey the land. But with the passing of the years the desert had widened and the grazing grounds had shrunk. The ancestor had withdrawn to the site of the present village and started a settlement.

There was a spear in the village which was said to have belonged to the ancestor who had fathered the village. Over the generations the spear had become a reminder to the villagers of their ancestor's courage and saintliness as well as the sacred importance of their own solidarity. Even now, five hundred years later, the tip of the spear glistened in the light, speaking eloquently of its maker's mastery with iron.

The spear was kept in the house of the village elder and brought out during important ceremonies. On days of celebration, remembrance, and thanksgiving, the head of each family would approach the spear, close his eyes, and touch the tip of the spear with his forehead.

Yet even more than the spear, they venerated Allah, the God that had been brought to them by travellers from Arabia many hundreds of years ago. The relative poverty and simplicity of their lives allowed them to stay on Allah's good side; there was no one in the village rich enough to trick or rob. Every family in the small village believed in its own innocence and remained convinced that its livelihood would always be protected by Allah.

*

But simple faith hadn't sufficed over the years. The land had gone its own way and changed in spite of the good intentions of its inhabitants. Mohammed's ancestors had managed to take care of their basic needs. Each village had always produced all the foodstuffs it needed. Yet things had changed when the foreigners had arrived and taught them to produce foods for export. Some regions had even stopped food production altogether. In the highlands, men who had once farmed and herded, now cut down trees and burnt them into charcoal for export.

And there had been other changes too. Years of excessive herding had exhausted the soil and made it more vulnerable than ever before to droughts. The herds had a cruel way of grazing. The camels, in particular, tore the grass up, roots and all, leaving the earth barren. Much land was needed to support a small herd, much more than what was needed to grow grain. As the herds grew in size, they were moved onto the farmlands until the farmlands themselves began shrinking, giving way to an ever wider desert. But herding was a tradition. It wasn't easy to convince a man to abandon the ways of his forefathers. It was a matter of habit, pride, identity.

*

Mohammed's house was a modest house. Although smaller and simpler than the houses owned by the merchants in the larger towns, it was enough for the needs of his family. The house was made of a mixture of straw and clay—the straw empowered the clay, acting much like the steel beams in the newer houses.

The house had been built by his father and his neighbours in a week. No sooner was the front door nailed to its hinges than the neighbours began a celebration to bless the house. The feast lasted all day and far into the night. The spear was brought into the house and each room was blessed with it. They danced for hours, never stopping the chanting, the flutes and the drums.

Mohammed's father had often retold the story of the building of the house and the kindness of his neighbours. And at every telling, he had clicked his tongue in wonder and gratitude.

A small clearing set the house off from the main road. In the middle of the clearing was a large tree that had been there longer than anyone could remember. It was believed that the carved words "Allah Akbar" on the trunk of the tree had been made by the ancestor himself. Mohammed felt privileged that the tree with the ancient carving was in front of his house.

To the left of the house and separated from it by a long fence of sticks was a large field. It was planted exclusively with potatoes. The field was owned by a rich merchant in Baidoa who imported machines from a company in Europe. Mohammed received a third of the harvest for his labour. Yet when the time came to sell the produce, the merchant received a higher price per kilo than Mohammed, because the merchant carted his share off to market in his own truck and needed no middlemen. Mohammed had to wait for the wholesalers who drove in from Baidoa. The merchant never offered to take Mohammed's produce into town for him, preferring to let Mohammed live out his lot and never save enough money to buy his own land.

Over the years, Mohammed managed to acquire a small herd. There were three goats and four head of cattle. The herd provided milk for the children. Sometimes an animal was used for its meat, but only when a newborn calf had grown mature enough to replace the animal picked for slaughter. And even then, the slaughter was done only on a special occasion when the meat could be shared with other families in the village.

Mohammed's village didn't consider itself poor. Every household managed to feed itself and keep aside enough grain to carry it through a year of drought. And since each family owned roughly the same amount, no one felt that nagging sense of poverty known by those who have enough but see others who have much more.

Most of the foreigners who came and went in this land never quite understood Mohammed and his kin. They mistook their ability to live in the present moment for lack of ambition, the innocent clarity of their eyes for lack of learning. In the earliest days of the occupation, they called them "uncivilized," not bothering to learn the proper pronunciation of their names or notice their aristocratic bearing, forgetting that the forefathers of these proud Africans had once invented the spears which the Romans later copied and used to conquer the world.

*

Mohammed waited patiently for his son to be old enough to join him in the field. He dreamt of the day when Ibrahim would be standing next to him just as he had stood next to his father. Arriving home every evening after bringing the herd back from the river, he would look at the little boy fondly, smile at Khadijeh, and remark, with an appreciative click of his tongue, "He will be a strong man. Look at his legs. They are already running to the next village."

Ibrahim was a contented child, as most children are when left free to roam in a place where there are fields, trees, water, and no large buildings to interrupt the wind. He spent much of his time at the river that flowed though their village. He would sit on its banks and close his eyes and listen to the unfaltering sound of the rushing water. And then, coming out of his reverie, he would jump into the cool river and swim against the current, glad that his legs were becoming stronger. He looked forward to the day when he would be old enough to work alongside his father.

There was a cooperation between child and parent in this culture that might seem odd to someone brought up on a steady diet of generational strife. Change had always been slow in this part of the world. What worked for the fathers and mothers continued to work for the children. So it was no miracle that the children had no pressing need to ridicule the habits of their elders; a strong bond of pride and respect existed between fathers and sons, mothers and daughters.

When Ibrahim turned ten, Mohammed began giving him greater responsibilities. Until then, he had carried buckets of wa-

ter from the well and tied together small bundles of firewood.
Now Mohammed gave him the responsibility of herding the animals. It was a rite of initiation that signalled to Ibrahim that he was
joining his father's world. He took the herding stick from
Mohammed's hand and nodded with pride.

And when the potatoes were ready for harvesting, Ibrahim followed his father through the mounds of earth and made a point of
picking the larger ones. It was a silly competition that delighted
them both. Mohammed looked at his son and murmured in his
mind, "Allah Akbar." His silent affection for his son ran deep in his
heart and joined his prayer of thanksgiving.

Mohammed's daughter, Aisha, was five years older than Ibrahim. As she grew into a young woman, she surprised Mohammed
and Khadijeh by taking on the height of the Somali women who
lived in the fiercely independent armed tribes of the highlands.

Aisha seemed to be the daughter of a more ancient and more
regal age. Sometimes when discussions between her father and his
friends became heated and risked turning bitter, she passed by
where they sat and the grace of her bearing cleared the air and re-
stored peace to the hearts of the men. And her mind went beyond
the customs of her culture. She was never disrespectful of the traditions of her elders, but there was a part of her that remained un-
convinced by some of their simple explanations. When they said
that the widening desert had been Allah's will, she couldn't help
noticing that when some of the animals grazed they took out the
grass, roots and all. And when they said that Allah would look after their needs, come what may, she remembered reading in the
newspaper that some agricultural experts had proven that grain
and vegetables could be grown on a fraction of the size of earth
needed for a herd. She couldn't understand why the country
wouldn't take heed and limit the ravenous herds. She wondered
whether Allah could be held responsible for the world if its inhabitants didn't become equal partners with Him.

Some nights when her family was fast asleep, she walked out of
the house, turned her attention away from the grieving earth, and

gazed up at the stars. She thought back to her ancestors who had inhabited greener plains under these same skies. In her mind, each star came to represent the departed soul of an ancestor. Proud men and women emerged out of the night sky and into Aisha's mind. She had no heart for anything that was without pride.

Mohammed felt himself truly blessed. He had a wife who had always been loyal and caring, a daughter who could read and write, who was old enough to have her own family, and a son who had grown devoted to him and the land, just as he himself had been devoted to his father and his land. Mohammed considered himself a wealthy man.

It wasn't surprising then that he didn't take to worrying when the sun continued shining day in and day out and no rain came to feed the thirsty earth. He and his village had been used to droughts. Their history was full of them. They would pass through this one, too, he thought.

Neither Mohammed nor his kin expected the events which were set into motion when he was forty-four and his son Ibrahim, barely sixteen.

*

Had it been just another of the droughts which periodically plagued their part of the world, Mohammed's village might have managed. But this was a pestilence far deadlier than any cruelty of nature. This was a creation of man.

It began with a terrible unease that was picked up by the dry wind and spread from one clan to another. The clans had been unhappy with the dictator's long and unbending rule. They felt cheated and coerced. There had been some new schools and hospitals, but not enough had been spent to help the poorer people make it through a bad year. The dictator could have created work for the population. He could have built roads and irrigation systems to help prepare the land for when the rains came again. But he did little of that. Instead, he bought armaments from foreign countries.

The fighting began over some small incident that could have

been overlooked for the sake of peace. But as in most wars, a small incident was all it took to unleash the all-out vengeance that was a long time coming. Word reached the dictator that some of his troops had been attacked in retaliation for a large town he had bombarded a few months ago with powerful state-of-the-art rockets. He brooded over what to do next. For a very long time he had felt angered by the persisting stubbornness of the clans. Unable or unwilling now to think of an alternative, he reached for his phone, called his generals, and ordered them to search for guns, seize them, and show no mercy.

The army followed its orders and then some. Being poorly paid, the soldiers couldn't avoid the temptation of also seizing food and other valuable things. And as their hearts closed to the meaning of their acts, they turned to settling old debts of hatred, spending their bullets without a second thought. The clans rebelled and fought back the despised government troops. Various warlords began vying with one another for control. And not long after, it became common for two opposing clans to turn their fire on one another at the end of a joint attack on government troops.

There was no central authority left. A civil quarrel that had previously been reined in by a delicate network of traditions, strained courtesies, and the coercive force of dictatorial rule was rudely unleashed. A man could leave his village now and not know what might happen to him if he met a stranger just a few kilometres down the road.

The African plain was turned into a killing field, alternately parched by the relentless sun and irrigated with human blood. Territory was conquered, lost, and reconquered. Villages were burnt and then other villages razed in vengeance.

Meanwhile, the land sickened with the blood spilled over it and thirsted for rain. But the rain did not come.

*

As was the custom during every drought, a village meeting was called by the elders of Mohammed's village. The head of each family declared how much grain and seed his household held in storage; it was a way of promising each other their loyalty and cooperation. They calculated that they could manage till the end of the year if they ate very frugally. There would certainly be malnutrition. Some of the weakest would die, as happened during all long droughts. But the majority would survive and regain their strength.

Mohammed returned from the meeting and called together his family.

"We will have to live on one meal of grain per day until things get better," he said quietly.

"Why is there a war?" asked Ibrahim.

"This war isn't our war," replied Mohammed. "It has nothing to do with the reasons for which my grandfather and father worked this land. It has nothing to do with us and we have nothing to do with it."

Aisha added, "It's about stories going back before all of us were born. But I'm not sure it's just that. If it weren't for the power-hungry warlords, perhaps the clans would leave each other alone."

Mohammed nodded appreciatively. He liked it when his daughter said these things which she had taught herself. It made him proud that she could pick up a newspaper and read it while he had to rely on the radio for the news.

Planting a new crop was useless now. There was nothing they could do but wait for the drought to end. Mohammed was used to working from dawn to dusk and he found it difficult to sit idle. One afternoon while he sat under the tree brooding over the stubborn heat of the sun, Aisha brought him his own father's old flute and asked him to play. Although he didn't have the heart for it, he played, knowing that this was his daughter's way of fighting back. He remembered a tune that his father had played for him when he was a child and he played it now for his daughter. Aisha closed her eyes, listened to the yearning in the music, and tried to forget that they had become prisoners of a barren land.

Every afternoon now, they huddled around the radio and listened to the news reports. It was difficult to piece together what was really happening. The news came from government sources and was carefully edited before being broadcast. The official reports talked of heroic government troops easily defeating rebel troops. But the truck drivers who passed through from Baidoa brought different reports. The president, although mightily armed, seemed to be losing his nerve.

One afternoon they were once again gathered around the radio when a man replaced the regular announcer and identified himself as one of the rebel warlords. His voice was hoarse with newfound power. He announced that the dictator had been run out of town once and for all. Then he paused for effect and added that the time for retribution had come.

That day the land was overwhelmed by a myriad of tribal squabbles dating back hundreds of years. Some of the dictator's soldiers gave up and returned home to their clans, bringing their guns with them. Others remained loyal to their deposed leader and continued fighting in the name of a government that no longer existed.

One thing soon differentiated those who bore arms from the rest of the population. The armed men didn't lose weight. Their faces continued to be lively and the muscles in their arms and legs stayed strong. The armed men took food away from the unarmed villagers at gunpoint. And then some of the food reappeared later on the black market, at prices that were far beyond the reach of those who had grown the food in the first place.

*

One afternoon, in the fifth month of the war, when traffic between the villages had been nearly strangled by the warring troops, a truck managed to arrive in Mohammed's village. Mohammed and his neighbours crowded around the truck and listened to the driver tell harrowing stories of famine. Thousands had died from hunger and many had started migrating on foot across the dry plains. The driver reported that, passing through one region, he had seen an enormous cloud of dust that seemed to stretch right across the horizon. Then, nearing the spot, he had seen thousands trudging through the burning desert in silence.

One of the villagers begged the driver to take his children to Baidoa and deliver them to their uncle. But the driver lowered his head and said that he might be shot by the troops if he did such a thing. He returned to his truck and sped away, furious that a man could no longer be true to his conscience without losing his life.

Mohammed walked back to his house and stretched out on a cot, too tired to think clearly anymore. For now, he welcomed the mindlessness of sleep.

But he awoke with a start an hour later. The butt of a semiautomatic rifle was jabbing his shoulder. "Wake up! Stand up!" commanded the soldier.

Mohammed stood up and tried to rub the pain out of his shoulder, but the soldier shoved him out of the room and out of the house. Ibrahim was standing next to the tree in the clearing. A soldier stood aiming a rifle at the boy's head. Another soldier pointed a machine gun at Khadijeh and Aisha who stood huddled together at the far side of the house.

Mohammed heard the sounds of distraught voices coming from the neighbouring houses. The same thing was happening at every other house in the village. Soldiers had been posted in front of each house and they had swung into action at an appointed moment.

"Where do you keep your grain?" asked the soldier imperiously. He had a gold tooth and it glistened in the sun.

"We don't have much," replied Mohammed.

The soldier's voice exploded with impatience: "Listen, old man, I haven't come here to count the number of grains. I want to know where you keep your food!"

Mohammed didn't answer. He knew that it was useless to resist. But delaying his response somehow helped him feel that he still had some freedom and worth as a man.

The soldier aimed his gun at Mohammed's head. "I'll give you ten seconds to tell me where you keep your food."

A shot rang out from one of the other houses. Khadijeh shouted: "Tell them, quickly. Don't be a fool. Give them what they want."

Mohammed glanced at his wife and felt ashamed that he didn't have the power to protect her and the children. He pointed reluctantly to a spot where he had dug a hole and buried a wooden box filled with two small bags of grain.

The soldier ran to the spot and took out a folding shovel from his backpack. He dug up the earth, uncovered the lid of the box and took out the two bags of grain. They were light enough to sling over one shoulder. He carried the bags to the truck and flung them carelessly in the back of the vehicle.

The soldier returned to where he had left Mohammed, aimed the gun at his head again, and ordered the soldier who was guarding the women to go into the house and fetch anything worthwhile. The second soldier emerged a few minutes later with a blanket in which he had thrown the few things that were worth keeping or selling. He walked over to Khadijeh and Aisha, unburdened them of their silver bracelets, and threw the bracelets in a canvas bag slung over his shoulder.

Satisfied that there was nothing more of value left, the soldiers climbed into their truck and drove away. Over the next few minutes, other trucks roared into gear and were driven away, until the only sound that could be heard was the wailing of the villagers.

*

There was just enough food left in the house for one meal. Khadijeh began preparing it as if nothing had happened. Aisha and Ibrahim followed her lead and began making a pot of tea. But there was a listlessness in their movements, the kind that moves in and numbs body and mind when there's no more good reason for hoping.

Mohammed was the first to speak: "They've taken all the food in the village. There's nothing left." And he began weeping with the helplessness of one who realizes that his life is no longer in his own hands. His sobs startled Khadijeh. She had never seen or heard him cry. She joined him and tore at her dress in mourning. And their voices rose to join the wailing coming from the other houses.

Next morning, Mohammed remembered his herd and felt a great relief. It wouldn't be easy to bring himself to slaughter the animals. But he would have to do it to keep his family alive. He went out of the house and walked over to the field. Normally he would have seen the heads of the animals, even if they were lying down. But arriving at the field, he saw nothing but parched earth. Another few steps and he was standing, legs shaking, looking down at what was left of his herd—small parts of the bony carcasses of the cattle, and as for the goats, they were nowhere to be seen. Mohammed knew that no one from the village would have done such a thing. Someone must have come with a truck in the middle of the night.

Khadijeh took one look at Mohammed's face when he returned and realized what had happened. She let out a curse. It startled Mohammed to hear his wife curse. She had never done it before. He nodded with respect and they looked into each other's eyes and shared their fear for their children's lives.

Mohammed told his family that they would have to go out beyond the farm and forage for food in the bush. Ibrahim fetched a pail and followed his father out of the house. Walking into the bush, they saw other villagers setting out on similarly desperate missions. It was an eerie sight. Small groups of men, women, and children moved in silence, searching for their life in a barren land, not knowing whether they would find any small remnant of it.

Making their way into the bush, they found holes in the ground where small animals had once burrowed. But the holes were no longer inhabited. Mohammed smiled with irony, thinking that the animals had been smart enough to flee.

Ibrahim found a plant with edible roots and tore it out of the earth and put it in the pail. An hour later, they found another small bunch of roots. But that was all they turned up the entire afternoon. They and the other villagers returned to their homes with nearly empty pails. Ibrahim handed the roots to his mother. There was just enough to prepare the pretence of a meal.

Mohammed had a bit of tobacco left hidden in a tin box that had gone unnoticed by the looters. He lit his pipe and went out of the house. He sat on a wooden crate, puffed on the pipe, and stared down the empty road wondering whether anyone would come to help.

Ibrahim came out and stood next to his father. Mohammed turned his eyes away from his son to conceal his worry, but not before he noticed that the boy had already lost weight. Mohammed had seen the starving who had poured in from Ethiopia a few years earlier. He shuddered to think that his son could soon end up resembling them. He shut his eyes and pleaded with Allah to intervene.

That week they had three meals. One was made from the roots they had gathered. The other two were made by boiling the bony remnants of the herd. At the final meal, Aisha stared at the pale soup in her dish and then stood up and walked out of the house. She knew it was their last meal ... she preferred to save herself the humiliation and pretend she'd eaten it days ago. She sat in the clearing, looked up at the stars, and forgot her hunger.

*

There was nothing for them to do now but begin the long journey towards death. Each of them was subject to the same universal physiological laws. First, there was a grumbling in the belly as the body released digestive agents in anticipation of food. Their stomachs burned with the acidity, and the burning continued as long as the body held out any hope of being fed. Then the burning was replaced by sporadic waves of nausea. There was the occasional headache as the sugar in the blood dipped to painfully low levels. There were also unnerving spasms that coursed through the body unannounced.

Each part of the body began thinning. Ironically enough, only the belly didn't lose weight. The bellies of the villagers began swelling with the water which their collapsing metabolism could no longer eliminate. And as the days wore on, upper and lower arms took on the same thickness, until the entire breadth of any part of the arm was not much larger than the wrist. There was a similar thinning of the thighs and legs.

The same physiological metamorphoses occurred in every house, as the village continued to starve. Only the sun, moon, and stars remained unaffected. The villagers, no longer strong enough to walk normally, shuffled around painfully on legs that were pitifully inadequate for the rugged terrain.

Each day they glanced at the road, hoping that a truck would arrive. Some thought of relatives living in nearby villages and prayed that they would come to their rescue. But help did not come. The roads were blocked by the troops of the warring warlords.

Each week brought them closer to the fulfilment of the death warrant left behind by the looting soldiers. No action was available to them except interminable waiting. They couldn't beg a meal from each other since they had all been reduced to beggars. For some, the helplessness turned into pain and rage. But most of them felt too feeble to feel any indignation. They lay in their houses or outside under some shade, absentmindedly swatting the flies that kept landing on their faces.

In the midst of this parched and desolate land they were no longer the centre of the earth. Life no longer took much account of them. They were at its mercy and it was turning its back on them. Looking into each other's faces, they saw reminders of their own approaching doom; faces had shrunk and eyes became enormous in comparison. It was as if the soul had fled the rest of the body and sought refuge in the eyes.

The grandmothers, grandfathers and the youngest of the children were the first to die. Mohammed felt thankful that his father had passed away years ago and wasn't alive to witness this terrible defeat.

One night, a man riding a bicycle arrived at the village. He went from house to house telling the villagers that the foreigners had come to Baidoa and were distributing food. He urged the villagers to try and walk the seventeen kilometres to Baidoa. Some swore they would attempt the difficult journey the next evening when it would be cool enough to travel; others, too weak even to stand up, sank back into their reveries.

Mohammed went to sleep that night determined that he would convince Aisha and Ibrahim to make the journey. He and Khadijeh were too weak to walk. But the children had to try. They were the only hope left. Lying on his cot, Mohammed remembered how much he had wanted to go on the pilgrimage to Mecca. He realized now that it would remain only a wish. Even so, he closed his weary eyes and saw himself and Ibrahim joining a throng of pilgrims circling the Holy Kabah Stone in Mecca ... closer and closer to the stone they worked their way through the crowd, and as they reached out to touch the Holy Stone, chanting "Allah Akbar!" in unison with all the other pilgrims, Mohammed awoke in a terrible sweat. The sounds of the praying voices in Mecca had been replaced with the distraught shouts of his neighbours. Mohammed stumbled from his cot and made his way to the tree in the clearing, and leaning against it, gazed down the road to the neighbouring houses.

Standing in front of the house of the village elder was a soldier in his early thirties, also two younger soldiers who looked as if they had been dragged out of school and outfitted with uniforms several sizes too large for their boyish builds.

Talking through hand-held megaphones, they ordered the villagers to assemble. Those who had been strong enough to stumble out of their houses when the jeep screeched to a halt now stood huddled together in front of the soldiers.

Mohammed wanted to hurry back into the house, but something kept him rooted to where he was standing. He feared some terror was about to overtake the neighbours he had loved all his life.

The oldest of the three soldiers looked with contempt at the emaciated villagers assembled in front of him. "Where have you hidden your food?" boomed his voice over the megaphone.

One of the villagers gathered his wits and dared to speak. "There is no food. You took it all away from us. You took everything. We have nothing left. You need only look at us to know that." The others followed his lead and nodded their heads.

The soldier let out a curse, turned to his two young assistants, and told them to search the houses. His assistants followed his orders, but found no food or anything else worth looting.

The older soldier paused to gather his thoughts, then gave a quick nod. The younger soldiers knew the signal. They had obeyed it many times before. They ran to the jeep and returned with cans of gasoline. Then they hurried from house to house, splashing the fuel on the sides of the houses and then setting the houses on fire. Mohammed stretched his arm forward in a gesture of protest, but there was nothing he could do. He heard the screams of those too weak to come out as they succumbed to the flames and smoke.

The older soldier then ordered his young assistants to go and sit in the jeep. Perhaps he felt proud that he would do this all by himself. The vengeance would be his alone. He thought of how he would recount this night to members of his clan, how proud they would be of his daring.

His lips twisted into a grin, triumphant, yet also frightened. A crazed yell escaped his throat as he squeezed the trigger of his machine gun and unleashed its furious bullets. He spun the gun in a wide unforgiving arc, until every man, woman and child collapsed in one screaming heap.

Mohammed turned to hurry back inside the house to warn his family. But Khadijeh and Ibrahim were already out of the house; the gun-fire had awakened them.

The jeep arrived an instant later. The older soldier jumped out and walked up to Mohammed, with a slow omnipotent swagger. His two young assistants followed, one of them carrying a can of fuel.

"Do you have any food hidden anywhere?" he demanded.

"Do you realize what you're saying?" asked Mohammed with a

bitter smile. "This is like throwing a man's identity papers in the fire and then asking him to prove his date of birth. You've already looted us. Now you come back to insult us?"

The soldier stepped forward and slapped Mohammed in the face.

Mohammed ignored the slap. "We have no food. We've forgotten its taste."

The soldier shrugged. "Some of the others had food." It was a lie, but he said it hoping that Mohammed might reveal the location of any hidden food in a bid to save his life. The ruse had worked in one village and he now used it as a standard question whenever he raided a house.

"We have none," repeated Mohammed, staring impassively at the soldier.

"How many are in your family?" demanded the soldier suspiciously.

"Just the three of us that you see here," answered Mohammed, hoping that Aisha would have enough sense to stay in the house.

"Just the three of you? A man of your age has only one son … " The soldier stopped in mid-sentence. Aisha had come out of the house. The thought of staying inside while her family stood outside had seemed cowardly to her.

The soldier's eyes travelled from her high cheek bones down her tall body. Even though she was starved and her legs nothing but sticks, she still appeared regal, self sufficient, and arrogantly attractive.

Something in the dignity of her bearing disturbed and insulted the soldier. The clear beauty of her moonlit face mocked his complicated hatred. The peace she carried in her emaciated body made him feel that everything was wrong with him. An ancient force had appeared in this murderous night to make him feel less than he imagined himself to be. His lips trembled for an instant.

"Not only is this a farm, it's also a brothel," he laughed belligerently, searching Mohammed's face for some sign of rebellion, for some new reason to slap it again. The two younger soldiers joined in the laughter, not knowing exactly why they were laughing, but sensing that their chief required it of them. Mohammed felt the blood rush to his head.

The soldier went back to staring at Aisha. "Come here," he ordered.

Aisha did not move. The soldier cursed and fired his machine gun, sending a hail of bullets a few feet in front of where she was standing. Still she did not move.

The soldier scowled at her silent negation of his power. Cursing, he ran to her, grabbed her wrist, and pulled her away from the house. Then he yelled to his young assistants to tie Mohammed to the tree.

The younger of the two soldiers hesitated for a moment. Less than half Mohammed's age, he had been raised to respect his elders. The thought of tying Mohammed to a tree struck him as the breaking of an ancient taboo, the rude insulting of his own father. But he followed the order. A rope was found and Mohammed tied to the tree on which his ancestor had carved the words "Allah Akbar" hundreds of years ago. Mohammed resisted for the sake of pride, but his strength had gone from him.

Khadijeh suddenly understood the soldier's intent. She tried quickly to draw his attention away from her daughter and back to her husband and herself: "How can you tie my husband to a tree?" she accused. "He is a Somali. And I am a Somali. How can you do such a thing to us?"

The soldier laughed raucously: "Your husband isn't a Somali. He is of this clan. My grandfather was killed by someone of this clan. So don't talk to me of Somalis. There are no Somalis left anymore ... and a good thing too."

Ibrahim couldn't understand why they were tying his father to a tree. If they wanted to kill his father they could shoot him right where he stood; there was no need to tie him up first. His heart was at once angry and afraid. If he were to advance on the soldier, he would be gunned down. Yet if he didn't say or do anything, he would feel humiliated. He tasted the meaning of powerlessness and it left a bitter burning in his swollen belly.

Mohammed choked back his tears and begged Allah to intervene. It was one thing to be robbed and slapped. But having his body exposed in all its weakness while his daughter was delivered into the hands of such a cursed man was the worst degradation.

The soldier moved his face close to Mohammed's and looked straight into his eyes. This was between him and the head of the family, a private humiliation to be delivered man to man, much like an arrow shot at pointblank range. "I'm going to take your daughter behind the house ... and then I and the other two are going to use her ... and you don't have the courage or strength to stop us," he whispered. And a look of contempt came over his face as he turned away from Mohammed and headed towards Aisha with mean measured steps.

A small part of him that had managed to remain clearheaded murmured to him that it was a hollow victory torturing those who had already been tortured by their own lives. But that part of him was all but drowned by years of arrogance, anger and hatred. A larger, more brutal side of the man took over. Eyes glazed, he closed in on Aisha, lifted her up, and carelessly draped her over his shoulder. Motioning impatiently to the two younger soldiers to follow him, he walked to the back of the house, and headed for Mohammed's hill.

Khadijeh tried to scream. But the scream reached only as far as her throat and froze there. She moved to the tree, put her arms around Mohammed, and leaned her frail body against his. Then something shifted in her mind. She stared into the night, seeing nothing, hearing nothing.

Ibrahim bowed his head and looked at his swollen belly. He felt ashamed even though he was innocent of all wrong doing. He moved closer to his father and mother and stood dutifully next to them. He knew that none of them had the strength to do anything for Aisha. He shut his eyes and prayed that they would bring her back alive.

The soldier hurried to the hill, carrying the defenceless girl over his shoulder. Had this been happening in a normal time, she would have felt mortified at the inevitability of losing her virginity. She would have thought of how difficult it would be to find a husband in a culture where a woman was expected to arrive at her wedding night still a virgin. In a more normal time, she would have had a husband already.

She knew she was starving to death and had very little time left. What difference did anything make now? Draped over the soldier like a cape, she felt numb and a little careless. If there were any emotion, it was embarrassment. This was the hill where her father had come to pray. She felt ashamed to have her nakedness revealed on this same ground that had been her father's sacred prayer rug.

The soldier threw her on the ground, turned to one of the younger soldiers, and said belligerently, "Do you think you're man enough for her? I bet on my grandfather's grave that you're still a virgin."

The boy went red in the face. He had never been with a woman before. He had planned to have his own family when the fighting ended and he could land himself a job in Baidoa or Mogadishu. The sprawled body of the frail girl wasn't of his choosing. He turned to the older soldier to protest, but saw the soldier pointing his revolver at him.

The boy advanced and knelt trembling in front of Aisha. He fumbled with his zipper and then fell on her. He moved clumsily and got off a few moments later, pretending to zip up the trousers which he hadn't unzipped in the first place.

"What's wrong?" demanded the older soldier.

"Nothing chief. I finished," lied the boy.

The older soldier laughed derisively. "I should have known you wouldn't be man enough." He pushed the young soldier aside and fell on Aisha. She felt a searing pain as his weight pressed against her swollen belly.

It irritated him that she offered no resistance. It was as if she were purposefully ignoring his presence. She remained an awkward reminder of what was wrong in him. He stared into her wide clear eyes and, hoping to elicit some recognition of his presence, stammered, "If you're nice, I'll take you with me to Baidoa ... where there's good food and drink."

He couldn't have found a ruder insult had he searched for one. His counterfeit promise awakened a proud rage in Aisha. Food no longer meant anything to her. She looked into the soldier's leering contorted face, inches away from hers, and saw the spirit of the beast that had taken over her people and decimated them.

His hatred now turned into some dark maelstrom that he mistook for lust. The two younger soldiers asked him to stop. They even took to pleading with him to pull away, for the sake of their own sisters, out of respect for them if nothing else. But his mind no longer heard them. Had he wanted sexual pleasure, he could have gone to any of the prostitutes in Mogadishu. But this was about humiliating a man tied to a tree and about breaking the spirit of a proud girl who was making him feel less than a man.

The rage surged through him and moved up into his head and down through his loins. And then he was mindlessly grinding his way into her. At first, she felt as if she were suspended in midair, being moved by some monotonous force. The weakness of her body created this merciful illusion.

But then Aisha remembered her grandfather and how hard he had worked to keep this land alive. She thought of her father who had helplessly watched it die, and her mother who had courageously comforted them all even though sorely needing comfort herself. What awakened in her now was something much more powerful than the grunts and thrusts of the man writhing in the dust. Suddenly the weakness brought on by months of starvation was gone from her. It was as if her ancestors reached out to her across the hundreds of years. It wasn't the scream of a woman suffering a brutal man, nor the wail of a woman calling for help. It was the death wail of a woman mourning her people. Every breath she took brought with it the strength needed for the next wail.

The more she thought of what had been done to her people, the louder became the chant-like screams that poured out from this hitherto unknown part of herself. With each thrust of the soldier, she wailed for a different person. She wailed for her father. She wailed for her mother and for her brother. She wailed in honour of her grandfather, in honour of her neighbours who had died there that night, in honour of the children that would never be born. She wailed for the ancestor who had come there five hundred years ago, and for the roaming clans who had once lived on the banks of the lush rivers. Her eyes burned with proud screams.

The soldier spent himself to exhaustion trying to block her voice out of his mind. Getting up, he glanced at Aisha's bruised body. It was still majestic beyond his comprehension. And it still wailed, long, loud wails that took no account of him.

He couldn't bear such humiliation any longer, and he snatched his knife from his military belt. As Aisha saw the sharp moonlit blade slice through the air, she gave one final cry, the cry of a young girl calling out to her mother, and then dropped quickly into blessed sleep.

The soldiers left her there on the hill and hurried back to the house. The older soldier walked up to Mohammed. Pushing Khadijeh aside, he hissed at Mohammed, "I could kill you and burn down your house, but I want you to stay alive and watch yourself die." He then paused for effect and added, "As for your daughter ... she was better than the best whores of Baidoa ... and I have known a few."

The insult was complete. The vengeance delivered in full measure. He and his assistants climbed into the jeep and drove off.

After a moment, Ibrahim went into the house and fetched a knife. Carefully he cut the ropes that tied his father to the tree. He rubbed his father's wrists and helped him back into the house. He didn't look at his father, nor his father at him. Then he went and brought his mother in. She shuffled to her bed and collapsed without a sound.

Telling Ibrahim to stay with his mother, Mohammed went out and found the can of gasoline left behind by the soldiers. He tied a rope to the handle of the gasoline can and then, pulling on the rope, began dragging the can to the hill behind the house. It took him half an hour to shuffle across the same distance that he had crossed in half a minute the night Ibrahim had been born.

He found Aisha's body spilled over on the spot where he had knelt to pray. He covered her with her shawl and stood next to her for a moment, his mind still and empty. There was a surprising peace on her face.

Too weak to dig a grave for her, Mohammed gathered all his strength and lifted the gasoline can. He poured fuel over his daughter, took a matchbox out of his pocket, lit a match, hesitated for an instant to steady his trembling hand, and then threw the match on her body.

He stood a few feet away from her and watched the flames fly up and flicker into the darkness. One red hot spark stayed burning much longer than the others until it too stopped glowing, lost its weight, and disappeared into the dark night.

Mohammed turned around, and moved away from the hill, with the slow and aimless steps of a man broken beyond self pity.

*

None of them said a word that night. They had all three heard her screams and understood their meaning.

Khadijeh lay on her bed and stared at the moonlit wall of the room. Even the best of men and women reach a point where all resistance leaves them. Khadijeh let go now and closed her eyes, neither seeing nor feeling. Her breathing slowed, became very faint and then ceased.

Early next morning, Mohammed limped out of the house carrying his wife's body, using what was left of his strength. He took her to the hill and burned her body just as he had his daughter's.

Afterwards at the clearing in front of the house, he eased his bony body down on an old wooden box. It was painful to sit on the hard surface; there wasn't enough muscle and flesh to soften the rubbing of bone against wood. Dizziness washed over him and he steadied himself not to fall off the box. His life was ebbing away—there was no question about it—he knew it. The entire landscape was ebbing away. Aisha and Khadijeh had been a part of him and they had been taken away. What was left of his life was leaving him too.

Mohammed looked in the direction of his field, squinting against the angry glare of the sun. There wasn't a shred of grass anywhere. The earth was mortally wounded, cracked open, begging for moisture, no longer able to serve the men who had once kept it alive. He thought back to his father and his father's father, the hundreds of thousands of hours of backbreaking work ... and how it had all ended so abruptly.

Mohammed had always been a religious man, but he couldn't help wondering now what kind of God would withhold rain for so long. And what kind of God would allow one man to pitch himself against another with guns bought from a third? If, as taught in the Holy Book, everything was the will of Allah, had Allah then willed this desecration?

Ibrahim came out of the house. He knew why his mother hadn't awakened with the light of day. When he felt her breathing stop the night before, a searing loneliness had washed over him. Seeing his father sitting in silent distress, he came and stood next to him.

Mohammed looked at his son tenderly. "We will survive this," he murmured. "You will see. Help will come. We will stay strong until it comes."

Mohammed wondered if the whole notion that Allah was in control of the earth wasn't just a silly wish. Maybe, he mused, Allah was really at the mercy of humankind. Maybe Allah had his hands tied, just as his own hands had been tied by the soldiers. Maybe Allah would lose his hold if the men of the world didn't keep each other alive. But then, he thought, perhaps this was Allah's plan ... perhaps Allah worked in strictly practical terms, like a painter who defaces a painting he's just completed in order to paint a better one instead.

"The important thing is not to think of your belly," said

Mohammed to his son. "And remember to spit often to keep your lungs clear. Help will come, you will see."

But the road in front of their house remained deserted. Except for the occasional sound of a beam collapsing in one of the burnt houses, the only sounds were those of rustling leaves. To Mohammed, the rustling was the feeble hiss of a dying planet.

There wasn't much to make one day different from another: no meals or work shifts to separate the day into measured parts. The only perceptible change was that each day Mohammed and Ibrahim became weaker. Had the weakening happened suddenly in one large instalment, it would have terrified them both. A man who is healthy and who wakes up one morning having suddenly turned into skin and bones sees the horror of what has happened to him. But when the thinning is gradual, the day comes when the man accepts his lot without rebellion. It was as if death had come and sat on Mohammed's land and was mercifully waiting for him to be as weak as possible so that the final parting would be painless.

Mohammed and Ibrahim spent their days in the shade of the canopy outside the front door of the house. And when the cooler night came, they moved indoors. They didn't talk much. What can men find to talk of when their bodies are near total collapse? Yet in spite of their shared silence, Mohammed felt his heart aching for his son. He felt deep shame seeing his son's rickety legs. This son he had prayed for had become a skeleton covered with skin stretched over desolate bone.

Mohammed regretted now that his generation hadn't fought back harder. He thought that they should have perhaps lined themselves up in front of the guns of the looters and become martyrs. Perhaps that would have shamed the looters into seeing the horror of what they were doing.

He understood now that he loved his son much more than convention had ever allowed him to reveal. It wasn't the custom for a father and son to hug each other too often. The father was always walled off a little from his family, solitary in his pretence of enduring patriarchal authority.

Mohammed knew that what was left of his strength was going out of him, once and for all. He could no longer feel his legs. Lying in the shade this particular afternoon, he felt a heady weightlessness, as if a gentle breeze would carry him off forever. He knew that there was little time left to reach out to his son.

He called Ibrahim to his side and motioned for him to bend his head down close to his. He spoke with a voice weakened to a hoarse whisper. "Ibrahim … there's much you don't know about our past … I had … hoped to take you over the plains on a long voyage one day … show you where … our people dwelt during the days when they lived on the banks of the wadis … I would have liked to take you … to the museum in Mogadishu … show you the clothing of our tribal kings and queens. Giants once roamed this land … you must remember this."

Mohammed stopped talking and waited a few minutes to gather enough strength to continue.

Ibrahim tried to see in his mind's eye what his father was describing. What he cherished most of all, even more than the images that appeared in his mind, was that his father was really talking to him. They were flesh of flesh and blood of blood, at one with one another in their weakness, neither of them lord over the other.

Mohammed continued: "You remember the spear that is our ceremonial spear?" Ibrahim nodded. "I took the spear from the chief's house after they set fire to the village. The inside of the house didn't burn and the spear stayed whole. It's under my bed now. Take it with you wherever you go … it will bring you strength. Keep it with you … and sell it to no one … for that is your heritage. That is all I have to give to you." For an instant it occurred to Mohammed that perhaps his son would die there too and that his words would prove useless, but he quickly pushed the thought out of his mind.

Ibrahim swore to take care of the spear and honour it. Yet this talk disturbed him, for it meant that his father was making ready to leave him. He looked down at his own bruised feet and wondered where those silly feet could take him even if help did come.

The air was warmer than usual that night, so they decided to sleep outside the house. Mohammed joked in a feeble voice: "Do you think that we will be safe from looters out here?" And, at that, both he and Ibrahim grinned, enjoying their irreverence towards those who had destroyed them. Mohammed gathered his strength and stretched out his arm towards his son. Ibrahim moved closer to his father, and, together, they fell asleep.

Morning found Mohammed more feeble than ever. Pain in his chest made breathing difficult. His body was again feeling weightless, and, this time, it felt as if the weight would never return.

Ibrahim noticed that his father's breathing had become very shallow. There remained one bottle of water from what they had set aside before the well went dry. Ibrahim poured a little of the water into Mohammed's mouth and urged him to swallow ... but Mohammed gurgled it out and motioned to Ibrahim to preserve it.

"What can I do for you, Baba?" asked Ibrahim.

Mohammed forced open his feverish eyes. "Nothing my son. You have been a good son ... sit with me ... keep me company while I wait for Allah's messenger ... sit with me."

Ibrahim sat with his father, feeling embarrassed that his own strength was holding out longer. He poured some water on his father's brow and waited with him.

Mohammed could no longer keep his eyes open, but he didn't stop thinking of his son. A spear wasn't enough to leave such a good son who was going to be left alone in the world. He needed to leave him something more, something that spoke the love that was in his tired heart. Mohammed prayed to Allah to give his lungs enough strength for just a few more words.

There was one very important thing that had remained in his heart ever since he had knelt at the foot of the hill and prayed for a son. He gathered what was left of his strength and whispered to Ibrahim: "I had always hoped ... to take you on a pilgrimage to Mecca ... but I wasn't able to ... I always hoped ... the crop would leave us a little extra money ... and we could make the pilgrimage together. If you are ever strong and have money ... go to

Mecca … make the pilgrimage to Mecca … since my father and I never went … I would be proud of you."

Ibrahim knew a very precious gift was being given him by his father. He lay his hand on his father's arm, but Mohammed didn't seem to be with him anymore. He bent down and put his ear to his father's chest; the heart was weak, missing a beat, and then starting again.

Mohammed didn't feel Ibrahim's head touch his chest. He had given his son all he had. He now gave in to his own breathing and tried to follow it to wherever it was leading. His body felt lighter than ever. The lightness reminded him of how he felt as a young man when he playfully ran after Khadijeh in the lily fields near her father's village. The old happy laughter rang in his ears now.

He became very still and waited for Allah's messenger to appear and draw the veil of forgetfulness over his mind. But the messenger did not appear. Instead, Mohammed suddenly found himself standing on the bank of an immense river like no other he had ever seen.

Then, from the mist of the rushing river, emerged two majestic figures. One was dressed in full ceremonial garb. He was the king of the Somalis, high regent of all the clans. And next to him was the queen of that same old proud land and she was also dressed in fine regal clothing. The queen approached Mohammed. And Mohammed's heart leaped for one last time as he recognized his beloved daughter Aisha and floated into her cool outstretched arms.

*

Ibrahim knew that his father had gone. He sat and stared into the silence of the hot day, a silence broken only by the ominous rustling of the leaves. He felt frightened and alone, but he bit his lip and got up to do what had to be done. He covered his father with a shawl and dragged his body into the house. He sat next to his father through that day and night and prayed. When morning came, he knew he was too weak to dig a grave for his father. Yet if he left him there, the soldiers would return and fling his body in an unmarked mass grave like the carcass of a chicken.

From under his father's bed, he retrieved the spear. Then he took the kerosene lamp that lay on the kitchen table and lit it. He walked out of the house, carrying the lamp and the spear. He turned back and threw the kerosene lamp through the front door. Then, reaching the tree in the clearing, he reverently touched the inscription the ancestor had made on the bark of the tree, and took one last look at the burning house that his grandfather had built.

Ibrahim, the seventeen-year-old son of Mohammed and Khadijeh, the brother of Aisha, spear in hand, began making his way to the town of Baidoa. He trudged along the road, leaning on the spear, using its strength as his strength.

It wasn't any kind of human walk. It was the slow shuffle of a crazed wounded animal. The spear took turns acting as his right leg and then his left. He watched his legs drag from one step to another. There was no feeling in them. They were like the legs of another, not at all the legs that he had known as a younger boy. He had no idea of how far he was from help. It didn't matter that much in any event. What mattered was staying on his feet for yet one more moment.

Once in a while he passed corpses on the side of the road. They didn't perturb him, nor did it occur to him that his body could be the next to fall lifeless on the pavement. The corpses just seemed to be there, as if a natural part of the new African landscape. In one place was an entire family that had sat down to rest and never stood up again. In other places there were solitary figures fallen on the parched earth, many of them young boys who had set out for the relief centres after burying their parents.

The bottle of water tied to his waist was empty now. The sun bore down on his frail body, pitiless and relentless with its cruel heat, making no allowances for his youth or infirmity. Ibrahim closed his eyes against the sun and lost all thought. His body moved another few steps, and then collapsed to the ground.

They found him lying on the road, barely alive, just outside the limits of the town of Baidoa. The Red Cross ambulance was transporting survivors to the food shelters. And had it not been for the spear lying next to him, he might have gone unnoticed. But the tip of the spear caught the light of the sun and the ambulance driver saw it.

They brought him to the shelter-clinic, put him on a cot and placed his spear next to it. They hooked him up to an intravenous feeding unit. For two days he stayed in a deep sleep. And when he opened his eyes, he remembered nothing. He stared at the wall and the wall seemed to be the beginning, middle, and end of his life. He felt no pain, no hunger, no fear, or desire. There was only the faint beating of his heart and the faded paint of the wall next to his cot.

The doctor spoke to him, but Ibrahim heard his voice coming from somewhere far away. The words poured into his mind and faded away.

The third day they placed next to his cot a bowl of the special food mixture they were giving to those making their way back into life. It was a porridge of protein and grains. But it had been so long since he had eaten anything that both the desire and habit had gone from him. He turned away from the bowl of food and continued to stare at the wall.

A few days later the nurse succeeded in having him swallow some of the food. Another couple of days and she convinced him to sit up and feed himself. He followed her directions, but said not a word. He ate at the prescribed times and then sat on his bed, fingering the amulet around his neck. The threads of the amulet felt good to his touch.

One day, into the third week, a group of United Nations observers visited the ward and stopped by Ibrahim's bed. He looked up at them with the wide eyes of the starved, all expression concentrated in the eyes, the rest of the face expressionless. His eyes touched one of the observers to the quick and the observer turned away feeling deeply ashamed.

The Dutch doctor who was taking care of him spoke to him every day, hoping that he would respond. Not knowing any

Somali, the doctor spoke to him in Dutch. The important thing was to keep talking to him, to keep him in touch with human sound. But Ibrahim stared back at the doctor and did not respond.

On the second day of the fourth week, Ibrahim touched his knees and noticed that there was some feeling in them. He rubbed his legs tentatively. And, as he felt the blood moving in him, something began stirring in his mind. He fingered the amulet around his neck and, feeling the familiar texture of the threads, he remembered his mother sewing by the kerosene lamp at night. He remembered his father and saw him pushing the plough in the field, weighing the potatoes, and delivering the landlord his share. He remembered the soldiers and Aisha's clear eyes.

And then Ibrahim pushed the covers away and swung his legs down over the side of the bed. He caught up his spear, leaned on it to steady himself and then slowly straightened up on his trembling legs, looking like a tired hunter back from a long journey in the bush. He turned in the direction of the Dutch doctor and spoke for the first time since arriving at the relief centre.

The Dutch doctor heard Ibrahim speak but didn't understand what the boy had said. He called a Somali intern over and asked him to interpret. Ibrahim repeated himself.

"What is he saying?" the Dutch doctor asked, glad that the boy had spoken.

The intern looked at the doctor, a puzzled expression on his face, "The boy must be feverish. He says he wants to know the road to Mecca."

In Transit

Someone was washing his hands in the lavatory. So he waited inside the toilet stall. The automatic hand dryer came on, one of those dryers that go on whirring forever, long after the user has left. He waited. When there was silence, he opened the door of the toilet and looked out. No one. He emerged from the stall, pulling his luggage carrier behind him. He glanced at the doors of the other toilets. All of the doors were open.

He hurried to take out his shaving kit, lathered and shaved, using long quick movements. He rinsed his face, dried it, took a comb from his pocket, and combed his hair into place. Looking like any other passenger at the airport, he left the lavatory with his luggage cart.

Any other time he wouldn't have minded shaving in front of a stranger, especially not in an airport. Men in transit did it all the time. In fact, he had shaved here every day, in front of this same lavatory mirror, in this very same airport transit terminal, for the last six years. But today he wanted to have some privacy.

*

Today is his birthday. He's turning forty-nine. He's passed 2,192 days in the circular confines of the Terminus One transit section of Paris's Orly Airport—and not even a prisoner's paycheck. He remains stuck in frozen transit between the tarmac and the shuttle bus to Paris.

He's lost count of how many times passengers have said the same words to him: "We are very sorry about your predicament.

We wish there was something we could do. We hate to leave you here and go."

It has felt strange speaking with them while cast in the role of an unfortunate. Once, he too had been a passenger, with rights like all other passengers. He had stepped off a plane, glad to feel the breeze on his face, confident and excited to be arriving, curious about where his life would lead him. Yes, he had been a passenger once and the hostess had called him *monsieur.*

But now the staff at Terminus One call him George, since many of them find his real name difficult to pronounce. Never mind, he likes it when someone calls him by any name, because it feels good to be reminded that he still exists as a man. The name George seems a good compromise to him, written identically in English and French, with just a slight difference in pronunciation.

Today, on his birthday, he decides that he will spend a little of what's left of the five hundred dollars with which he arrived at the airport six years ago. He'll buy himself a pastry at the cafeteria, maybe one of those expensive chocolate pastries which he has seen behind the glass counters but never bought because of his constant fear of being left penniless. He feels safer knowing there's some money left in his pocket. The remaining few dollars give him the sense that he's still a man with the ability to make transactions.

*

He speaks very little French and the airport doctor who has befriended him speaks very little English. Even so, they have managed to forge a friendship composed of warm smiles and gestures. But he aches to speak with all his mind. He wishes he were in a country like Great Britain where everyone speaks English.

Great Britain. He had seen it on film when he was a young boy, loved its green spaces and plentiful rains. Perhaps his love for Britain had also something to do with the way in which Britain was regarded in his country when he was a little boy. He was born in a region under British administration, where everything British was revered by those educated in Western ways and held in awe by many of those who were not. People who spoke English were looked upon as if they possessed some special key to the future. And if one couldn't afford formal English lessons, then one subscribed to Reader's Digest and used a dictionary to read its simple condensed stories. The British clubs, the Anglo-Petroleum Company that sucked the crude oil out of the ground and syphoned it into the tankers, the British Council that lent English books and offered English classes according to the Cambridge method, and the American Armed Forces stationed there when he was a teenager—these things left a deep impression. So when time came for him to go to university, he chose London.

He wasn't the first or the last to feel this way. This habit of assuming that everything foreign was better than anything local had been taught to the population long before he was born. When his own father was a young man, the monarch of the country passed a law decreeing that all men had to wear western suits and western shoes. The men complied with bewilderment, afraid of being thrown in prison.

And there were other things that impressed him deeply when he was a child. He loved standing mesmerized on the crowded streets to watch for the monarch as he was driven from one place to another, flanked by his retinue of body guards. The hairs on his arms would stand on end when the royal guard mounted on their Harley Davidsons would roar down the boulevard, the leonine roar of the powerful engines signalling the impending arrival of the king. There would be a siren and, moments later, the monarch's black Rolls Royce would roll down the road. The applause of the crowd would rise to a deafening roar. Meanwhile, security men dressed in plain clothing would walk through the crowds, searching for suspicious faces, alert to the odd voice that might mumble a complaint or a curse.

He would crane his neck to see past the thick crowd, hoping to get a glimpse of the king as he waved to everyone benevolently. Sometimes, people would line up and wait at the boulevard for hours, never knowing when the monarch would arrive, because his arrival would be purposefully delayed to throw off possible assassins. He didn't mind the delays. He liked the way his neck and arms tingled while he waited for the motorcade to arrive. He would listen intently for the distant sound of the powerful motorcycles. And then the thunderous sounds of the machines would roar through the air and their roar would feel like the sound of hope itself.

One day his uncle sat him on his shoulders and he saw the king's face clearly. The king appeared to be waving in his direction. He felt certain that he had waved specifically at him. Had he known that one day, as a grown man, he would be put in prison on charges of being an enemy of this same king, the little boy in him might have burst into tears and run up to the motorcade and promised that such a thing would never happen. Great was the respect that many in his country held for this king who promised lifelong loyalty to the anonymous crowds while stocking numbered bank accounts in distant countries.

He also loved the movies that came from Britain and America. They showed a wonderful new world and promised that anyone could get anywhere if he only put in the effort. At first, when the stars in the movies kissed, the men and women in the audience shifted uneasily in their seats. They still lived in a culture where men and women didn't kiss each other on the lips unless near marriage, and even then not publicly. But with the passing of the years, the uneasy shifting turned into shy giggles as the lips of the stars clamped together. And then the giggles eventually faded away as many in the audience took to holding hands and rubbing knees.

As he grew past childhood and was sent across town on errands, he felt irritated with shopkeepers who always made you return, day after day, promising to have whatever needed repairing ready the next day. Things in the Western movies were quicker, less complicated. But where he lived, there wasn't much hurry. When the promised day arrived the shopkeepers would excuse themselves and repeat the same promise. "Go today, come back tomorrow," was a refrain jokingly traded between all citizens who had ever experienced the despair of dealing with a repair shop.

So he grew up thinking that the West had become all that it was because it did things on time. Once he saw on a television programme a report on the Big Ben clock in London, how it was regulated to the closest second and revered by Londoners who set their clocks by its faithful chimes. Everything seemed so organized and efficient there; people were methodical and patient even when they queued up. So he came to think that efficiency and goodness went hand in hand.

*

He points to the chocolate pastry. His finger hesitates, then points firmly.

"You know this is extra," reminds the woman behind the counter. "The pastries aren't covered in the meal ticket."

"I know," he says. "I'm going to pay for it."

The woman raises an eyebrow, surprised that he's spending money without worry. She puts the pastry on his lunch tray along with the daily special. He hands her the meal ticket, digging in his pocket for the price of the pastry.

He sits at a table, with his luggage carrier next to him, and begins eating his solitary meal. In his own country, he might have heard his family say many times over this day, "*Eydeton Mobarek Basheh,*" which translates: "May Your Birthday Be A Blessed One."

He eats the food, feeling grateful to the hostesses and airline pilots who pass him their meal tickets. He bites on the pastry, savouring it, swirls its voluptuous cream in his mouth. In his mind, he repeats, *Eydeton Mobarek Basheh.*

*

Journalists. There had been scores of them. As soon as the news had spread that a man had been in the Paris airport for nearly six years, newspapers and magazines had sent their reporters to cover

43

his story. A couple of the journalists wrote that he seemed to be enjoying his celebrity status, not realizing that a man might prefer to remain anonymous but free. He was screening the journalists now, trying to protect his story from distortion. He asked the journalists to be kind enough to send him a copy of the article they wrote about him. The ones who complied sent their envelopes care of the airport terminal. That was his legal address, after all.

It was a real test of nerves living in a public place while creating small semblances of privacy. Sometimes he would sit in the small non-denominational chapel in the terminus. But even though the chapel remained deserted most of the time, it still felt public, very different from a room of his own.

He had his choice of dozens of benches in the basement lounge, yet he eventually settled on one particular bench as his sleeping berth. Using one bench all the time created the illusion of a space that belonged to him alone, some constant resting place to which he could return after another day spent wandering the circular halls of Terminus One.

One time, a Texan in transit struck up a conversation with him. The man wore a pair of wonderful black motorcycle boots. He asked the Texan if he owned a motorcycle and the man replied that he owned a Harley Davidson that he used on weekends to burn off the stress of an executive life. The man obliged him by showing him a wallet-sized photo of the beautiful machine. "That's my chrome princess. It's a lot cheaper than a psychiatrist," he said. But the conversation came to a sudden end. The Texan gave him his business card, told him to call if ever he was in Houston, and rushed off to catch his connecting flight.

Many people had taken to giving him their calling cards after having these in-transit conversations with him. He had an entire box filled with these small reminders of the world that continued to exist beyond the limits of the transit lounge. It did him some good to emerge from anonymity and talk with a traveller. But every time, partway through the conversation, he would remember that the passenger would be on his way soon and that he would be left behind in Terminus One. He had lost count of how many times he had waved goodbye.

*

The hundreds of calling cards are tucked away in the boxes that contain the 6,000 pages of diary he's written since arriving at the airport. He writes almost every day: his thoughts, observations, emotions and descriptions of the people he meets. The diary gives him a way to put some variety in the days that follow one on the heels of another, days in which the same halls are seen, the same series of doors, the same shops, the same cafeteria counters, the same floor-buffing machines that arrive at all hours of the day and night.

Today he starts a new page in his diary and writes that it is his birthday and that he has eaten a voluptuous pastry. Then, setting his pen aside, he turns his mind back to his family's house and re-members the smell of the roses blooming in the garden each spring ... remembers the colourful dresses that his cousins wore each March 21st to celebrate the arrival of the New Year ... and the streets that were decorated with a riot of colours as the tradi-tional green plants were taken from house to house as harbingers of good luck for the coming year.

*

I noticed him walking in the terminus, pulling his luggage car-rier behind him. I had chosen Paris rather than Amsterdam as a transit point, hoping that I might catch a glimpse of him.

I called out his real name. He turned and smiled politely.

"Yes, I am he. How do you do?" he said. He was wearing a white, long-sleeved shirt and a pair of corduroy trousers. I had read in a news article that the corduroy trousers were given to him as a gift by a visiting journalist.

"How do you do?" I said. "I've read about you. I'm on my way to New York. I'm a writer. I'm not with a newspaper and I rarely publish in newspapers. Would you mind if we talked?"

"What do you write?" he asked warily.

"I know you must be suspicious. So many journalists have come already. I write books. I'm a novelist and I also write short stories and travel accounts."

"What are your novels and stories about?" he asked politely.

"This year I wrote a book about how people lose hold of their lives when governments stop caring about their own people."

"Well, as you can see I am not one of their own people here," he said, smiling with irony.

"Yes, but still, you've been kept in this airport for six years. That's like a prison term."

"They don't see it that way," he said, raising an eyebrow and shrugging with the world-weary resignation of a man who has stared into the face of unblinking stupidity. "They say I can't enter France but am free to go to any country that takes me. Problem is ... there's no country that will take me. There's nowhere left for me but this transit lounge ... neither here, nor there." He smiled at the biting accuracy of his last phrase; I think he felt proud to have thought of it.

"What about your own country?"

"I no longer have a passport from my own country. I was put in jail when I returned to my country after my university studies in London. When they let me out, they took my passport away and gave me a paper that allowed me to leave but never to return as a citizen."

"Who put you in prison? Why?"

"I was accused of being an enemy of the king ... because of my politics. I graduated in England with a degree in Slavonic studies."

"How long were you in prison?"

"It was long enough," he answered, glancing away.

"Yes, but your king was deposed. Wasn't your status revised when the government changed?"

"I was already in Europe. I didn't go back."

"Didn't you ask your embassy for a passport?"

He didn't answer.

I couldn't help wondering if all the details of his story were accurate. A journalist who had interviewed him had said that he showed no desire to return to his country and preferred to be allowed to enter England and complete his post-graduate studies. A highly-placed charges-d'affaires at his embassy confirmed that he would have readily been given a passport had he asked for it. The embassy reportedly even sent some people to talk to him, but nothing came of it. Nevertheless, these contradictions didn't lessen the pain that I felt for him. He seemed a humble man, unassuming, almost disturbingly gentle.

"So where did you go after you left your country?" I said, allowing him to continue with his own version of the story.

"I came to Europe. And then I went to the European High Commission for Refugees in Brussels. I explained my situation to the Commission and it accepted me as a refugee and gave me papers."

"Wouldn't that have allowed you to enter France?"

"Yes, in the new Europe, papers are good almost everywhere. But I lost the papers. I had them in my suitcase and the suitcase was stolen."

"Didn't you get replacements?"

"I reported the loss to the police and they gave me a written report of the loss. I went to the airport and showed the report to the airline. They sold me a ticket. When I arrived here in France, the immigration officers said that I couldn't come into the country because I didn't have papers. I explained what had happened and showed them the police report, but they continued to say I couldn't come in. They looked for somewhere to deport me ... but there was nowhere ... so they left me here in this terminal."

"But you don't even have a room of your own here," I protested.

"I know. It's difficult. It's like being in a bus station waiting years for a bus that never comes. I sleep on a bench in the basement lounge."

My temples were taut with anger. "How can you stand it?" I asked.

"I meet people. Some are very nice. The airport doctor is kind to me. Last year when I lost my cassette player, he bought me a new one with a built-in radio. The pilots and stewardesses are very nice too. They give me their meal tickets so I can eat at the cafeteria."

"You mean the authorities haven't arranged a meal plan for you?" I asked in bewilderment.

"No. You see, I am not a prisoner or anything. So I'm expected to be responsible for myself," he answered, logically, with the calmness of one who has come to understand that it is the letter of the law and not its spirit that rules the world.

"Do you have any money of your own left?"

"I had five hundred dollars when I arrived. But not much is left now."

"What about a lawyer? Is someone trying to end this nightmare for you?"

"I have a French lawyer who handles my case without charge. He's doing his best."

"Did he present your case in the French courts? What were the results?"

He looked at me a little puzzled, as if I had asked a silly question. "The law is the law. No papers—no entry. But at our last court appearance, they said they would let me go to Brussels for a few days to apply for refugee papers again."

"And ... ?"

"I didn't go. I was afraid to be kept at the airport there. I've become used to this airport. I don't want another one."

"But what will happen with all this? You can't grow old here. Your life is ebbing away."

"I would like England to take me in," he said. "That would be an honourable solution. I was educated there. I speak English. I don't speak French. It would be good if England gave me papers. I would like to be in England." When he said the word England, his face lit up, as if he were calling on some trusted childhood guardian, confident that he would come to the rescue.

"And what do the British say?"

"I don't know. I don't think they have said anything yet."

"What will happen next?" I asked, knowing it was a useless question, that we had arrived at a dead end.

"Tonight I will sleep on the bench, and tomorrow morning I will wake and go to the public lavatory, shave and wash my face, then have some tea and write in my diary." He pointed to the boxes tied to his luggage carrier. "I've written over six thousand pages."

I had some cash with me. I put my hand in my pocket to give him some. It seemed to me that it would bring him a relief far greater than any loss on my part. He saw my purpose and said quickly, "Please, no. This is the reality. It must stay this way until my situation is settled. I found two wallets filled with money and I turned them in to the security office. Money isn't the answer."

Our eyes locked. There was no great complaint in his eyes. I would have expected him to have taken on the hurt and angry look of a martyr after six years of monotonous wanderings in the wilderness of Terminus One. But there was a strange peace in his eyes. Even so, I felt bereft and my own eyes flooded with tears.

"I feel helpless. It's not just your situation. It's the whole world," I said.

"Ah, these people will be here long after you and I are gone," he said philosophically, almost as if I were the prisoner needing consoling and he the soothing visitor. "There's no way to win. You have to wait, patiently, until they decide to give you a few crumbs when they're good and ready. I told my lawyer that it will continue like this until they suddenly decide to let me go through those gates one day, without any explanations or apologies."

Then he said, "You know, where I come from, we have some folk tales that are attributed to this strange, funny sage who lived hundreds of years ago. His name was Hodja. Let me tell you one of the stories if you're not in a hurry. One day Hodja was called to preside over a court case. Feeling overwhelmed by the task, he decided to follow the safest path possible. The prosecution presented its case. Hodja listened and then said, 'You're right.' Then the defence presented its case. Hodja listened and again said, 'You're right.' The court clerk went up to Hodja and whispered to him, 'Hodja, this is a courtroom. You must pass judgement. They both can't be right.' Hodja thought for a moment and replied to the court clerk, 'You know, you're also right.'"

He shook his head and smiled. "You see? This is the way the world works. It all depends on your point of view. The judges in the court must have been convinced they were doing the right thing denying my pleas. I'm sure they didn't lose any sleep over it. And the population who heard of my case must have felt right not registering a protest. And you must feel right being indignant. I guess everybody's right."

It was difficult to say goodbye to him. I felt as if I were leaving a man to drown in a river to which I had no access. But there was nothing to be done about it. My plane was leaving in another few minutes and I had to go to the gates. I wanted to turn back and wave at him and shout something encouraging, but I couldn't bring myself to do it. I continued staring straight ahead until I was past the gates and on the plane.

I kept my eyes closed as the plane taxied away from the terminus. Usually I like to look out the window and watch the airport buildings as the plane pulls away. But this time I kept my eyes closed.

The Forbidden Zone

They said Sarajevo was dead, or dying at least. The world mourned that the city would never be itself again. But which Sarajevo were they talking about? The one that was there before the well-to-do packed up their belongings and left? Or this new city of unlikely stories, this ramshackle town glued together with the resolve of those who were either too poor, too patriotic, or just too terrified to leave?

I cared nothing about politics, nor notions of patriotism. Neither did I have any desire to save my neck and leave the country. I admit that, at some point, I even stopped caring whether the cursed city survived or not.

Even so, there were times when I admired the risks people took to remind themselves that they were still alive. Like the iron sculpture of a bicyclist that appeared one morning at dawn, exactly where no one would ever have expected it to be. There it was, perched gloriously on a cable stretched between the banks of the Miljacka River. That very same afternoon, one of the students from the Sarajevo Art Academy took credit and explained to a bewildered television crew from France: "We put it up just like that for the hell of it, just for the sake of seeing whether or not we could do it at night, when they can't see us. And why the hell not, when we get off on it!"

And why the hell not? I had to laugh. It was me, after all, that they had fooled. The whole thing happened during my lookout, right under my own nose. I woke the morning after they put it up and took up my position just as I did every day. And then, looking out the window, I saw the thing perched in midair, thumbing its nose at the whole of Sarajevo. I was flabbergasted. I thought I was hallucinating. The thing seemed to have materialized from outer space. I could have taken it personally and despised them for getting away with it, but for some reason I didn't. Doing it at night so I wouldn't see them moving in the dark shadows, setting up their complicated wires and cables. It was a big sculpture after all. Nothing to laugh at. A bicyclist of all things. It was no joke to set it up on a cable in the middle of the night. It dawned on me that I had been tricked, good and proper. I doubled over laughing. I hadn't laughed like that in a long time. Yes, it was as if a midget had brought down a giant.

But please don't misunderstand me. Had I seen them doing it, I would have shot them instantly, without the slightest remorse. They would have received no special consideration. I would have aimed my rifle carefully, precisely, held my breath, pressed the trigger, and gone back to breathing easily again. My job was to shoot and not to miss. And I did it well.

I worked from a two-room apartment on the fourth floor of an abandoned highrise building. It overlooked the boulevard that separated our side from the besieged Muslim historic quarter. The press called it *no man's land*. I preferred to think of it as *the forbidden zone*.

I could see the entire forbidden zone from the window of the apartment. I could even see the open air theatre in the Muslim sector. My friend Meho and I used to go to a teahouse right next to the theatre on warm summer evenings. But after the barricades went up, he got stuck on his side of town and I on mine.

I liked working alone in the abandoned building. I was never one for teamwork. Before the war broke out, I worked as an apprentice mechanic in the city of Dubrovnik, on the Adriatic Coast. That was when Yugoslavia existed and all the towns along the coast were teeming with tourists. It was back when we still lived under the influence of the hammer and sickle. Things had to be done in committee. If a car wasn't working, half a dozen of us would gather around the engine and discuss what could be wrong with it, each doing his best to stay clear of a quick solution. Anyone who thought of a smart solution had to keep his mouth shut, not to appear too ambitious.

I was working as a mechanic to save money. I wanted to meet a woman, marry and have children. But after the war broke out ... well, it's hard to marry after you've seen so many women raped.

I didn't want to go to the war. But how to avoid it when you're sent a notice ordering you to report? My sister Anna begged me not to go. She wanted to hide me in a hole under the house, just as one of our neighbours had done for her son. But I couldn't see myself crouched for months on end in some damp hole. So I took my chances and reported to the induction centre.

The army was big on teamwork, too. Our commandants liked us doing things in bunches. One day we were ordered to burn houses. Another day to rape women ... so they would lose face with their neighbours and abandon their homes and move on to another region. During one assignment, I was sent to the town of Banja Luka where thousands of refugees were being herded onto sealed cattle trains bound for central Bosnia. I overheard the town's police chief talking to some foreign journalists who had come to witness the deportation. He referred to the forced migration as "safe transportation for those who wish to emigrate." The deportees were required to obtain twelve different certificates before being shipped out. They even had to get a certificate from the library attesting that they had no overdue books.

I hated their team spirit. Such mediocre nonsense wasn't my style. I wanted no part of their schoolboy games. Anyway, the way I see these things, if you're going to end someone's life, better do it quickly, preferably without them knowing. I wasn't a cheap torturer.

I came to envy my friend, Ratko. He worked as a sniper and didn't have to put up with any of their gang rape nonsense. I used to visit him in the apartment where he was stationed. It struck me that his work was a lot cleaner than what the regular army did. I mean, with all the signs and barricades everywhere, anyone entering the forbidden zone knew they shouldn't be there.

I was there in the room, talking to him, when he was brought down by a sniper from the other side. He went speechless in the middle of a sentence, looked like he was searching his mind for some word he'd forgotten, and fell over on his side ... just like that.

I hurried to the commandant and asked for Ratko's job. He asked why I wanted to replace my friend. He wanted to know if I hoped to avenge Ratko's death. Imagine, what a stupid question. What use to avenge anyone's death when you've lost track of the death count? No, I told him, I just wanted to work alone and do what had to be done. He then said some inane thing about how heartwarming it was that the nation's youth were coming together to defend the security of Serbia. Hell, what was he on about? I was no patriot. As far as I was concerned this had never been a country that could shoulder patriotism with a straight face. I mean, you can't stick three countries together and then ask everyone to pretend it's all in one piece—not people who still remember what they did to each other years ago.

Anyway, they gave me the job and set me up in a two-room apartment in an abandoned bombed-out building. There was a cot with a mattress, a pillow and a blanket. I also had a small propane stove, some candles, a towel, a bar of soap, and a small portable radio. I didn't wear an army uniform; blue jeans, T-shirt, sweater, and running shoes suited me fine. Every day two soldiers walked up the four flights of stairs and left me a box of food. Two sandwiches—one made of beef kebab with onions and turnips in it, a second one made of some chicken—a large bottle of mineral water, another of soda pop, and a pack of cigarettes. That's what it cost them to keep me. Not much, but more than most people in Sarajevo had to eat, even on their best days.

At first, I stationed myself at the window of the front room, just as Ratko had done. But then I realized that the snipers on the other side might easily see me. That's the mistake my friend made. He became cocksure and forgot that a sniper must remain totally invisible. But I used my head. I went into the bedroom and cut a hole in the wall large enough to stick out the rifle and its scope. I then smashed the glass of the window in the front room and left some of the shards in the frame. This made it look as though the apartment had been hit by a shell. I positioned myself behind the wall separating the bedroom from the living room. I felt good in the cocoon-like space of the inner room, an invisible man doing what he wanted without having to explain himself to anyone.

Staying invisible wasn't the only part of the job. I also had to make sure that the target itself didn't remain hidden. Sometimes I couldn't see the target and had no way of knowing where it was. But I knew it was there somewhere, that it was moving, and that it would get to where it wanted if I didn't react quickly enough. So I thought of a way to see the target even when it was too far to be visible. If it was a sunny day, I would concentrate on an area where I suspected movement. I'd wait for a burst of sunlight reflected off a button, belt-buckle or eyeglasses and would quickly shoot at the burst of glitter in the distance.

My mother died a few months ago. Nothing to do with the war. She climbed a ladder to reach something and her heart stopped. My father wasn't alive to bury her, so, being the only son, I went back home for the funeral. Six months before I might have cried at her burial. But after so many dead, it seemed maudlin to cry, almost out of place. My sister Anna wrote me a couple of weeks later begging me to return, complaining that she was all alone now and very worried. Again, she offered to hide me somewhere until the war was over. But I didn't answer her letter. I seemed to have crossed some invisible border.

A bicyclist hanging on a cable stretched across the sky, pedalling in empty space, trying to cross over from one hopeless side to the other. There's nothing silly in that. It's about the will to survive and all the little decisions people have to make here every day to keep body and soul together. Every minute a new question needs answering. Shall I risk going out to fetch water? Which route shall I take? Shall I stand in the market like a sitting duck just to buy a loaf of bread? What will I eat if I don't go out to buy the bread? How shall I send word to my brother in the next village? How to look my aunt in the eye when she and I both know that she was raped last week? The closer you are to annihilation, the more questions there are.

But I myself had few questions left. I liked being in the apartment, on my own. I could have lived somewhere else and come here just to put in my shifts. But I preferred staying here day and night. It helped me keep others faceless and nameless. The fewer faces I saw up close, the more anonymous I felt. There was a certain freedom in that. After all, isn't the executioner always brought out at the very last moment? Doesn't he always wear a hood?

I know you're probably thinking: "He's just a cheap murderer. What story could he have that's worth telling? Why listen to him? It's the incoherent babble of a psychopath. After all, doesn't he just kill people without even a warning, without the benefit of a hearing?"

I wish it were as simple as that. But you're never the same after a few months of war as you are in the beginning. A lot of meanings change. A murderer does what he does out of feeling. But after awhile, the anger and hatred turn into something else. You become a machine that's positioned to make sure life doesn't continue. There's a difference between terminating life and not allowing it to continue. It's a subtle difference, but it's there nonetheless.

It was very difficult the first time I killed a man. What man in his right mind could feel otherwise? I tried to aim the rifle, but my whole body began trembling as if it were diseased; my legs threatened to collapse. Then a second fear took over and washed away the first. I realized that I had to hurry, steady my hand, and shoot straight if I were to hit him before he hit me. I felt a rush of energy I'd never known before and it pushed me forward, pulled the trigger for me. Then it was too late ... it was done ... I was alive and relieved.

And why shouldn't it be like this the first time? Your hand isn't used to doing such things. Why expect it to jump into the thing

without faltering? Once the trigger explodes, the thing
your hands. Then you feel you've smashed some ancien
You break out into a sweat. You wonder if it's really happened or
whether you were only dreaming. You do anything to take your
mind in some other direction.

Some of my friends told me that, after their first time, they
prayed to God—as if God were some vaccine you took after the
first time to prepare you for the following times. Some others told
me they went to the movies or got drunk and turned their terror
into lusting rage. It takes time no matter how you handle it. Your
mind needs to come up with its own good reasons for going on.
My first time I sat on the ground and didn't move for a couple of
hours. I ran through my mind every injustice that I or anyone else
had ever experienced. When I stood up, it felt okay to go on.

After a few more times it turned into something that was separate from myself. It became a matter of skill—shooting at a moving target at just the right instant. A part of me turned the other
way so the rest of me could do what it had to do. It was rather like
those shooting games in the amusement parks, the ones where the
ducks are moving quickly and you're trying to bring down as
many of them as you can. One day I sent a rain of bullets on a
huge water pipe. I knew that I wouldn't get the man hiding in the
pipe. Still, it amused me to imagine the noise this made in his
head. Later, it shamed me to think that I had toyed with him like
that. As I said, I am not a torturer.

When I first sat at this window, I told myself that maybe I was
getting rid of those who had done us great wrongs many years
ago. Some days, I even felt like a sort of hero. But I got used to the
proud hatred after a while, or it got used to me and became part of
my breath and blood and lost its meaning. I began seeing myself as
more of a marksman than anything else.

Two soldiers dressed neatly in uniform brought me a medal one
night. They also gave me a bonus basket of food. There was some
fruit, two jars of jam, a long sausage, a package of crackers, three
cans of soda pop, six packs of cigarettes, and a plastic disposable

lighter. I pretended to be grateful for the medal and placed it on my pillow. I waited for them to leave and made myself a snack of sausage and crackers. Finishing the meal, I relaxed with one of the foreign cigarettes included in the gift basket. Then I leaned over and threw the medal out the window.

Medals always make me think of leaders. They love to give medals, as if we were dogs waiting to be rewarded with biscuits. You have to learn to survive in spite of them. Just this winter the leaders issued an edict. They said that all cars running on the roads in Sarajevo had to be equipped with winter gear: chains, snow tires, shovels, windshield cleaner. Imagine a man hurrying to get his car past sniper fire, having to stop at a checkpoint to show his proper equipment, all according to regulations. So the people found a way to get around it; the drivers would show their winter gloves to the policemen and the policemen would wave them on. This city hasn't survived *because* of its top officials, but in spite of them. So what does a medal mean to me.

And then there were the heroes of the media, the select cases carefully chosen to put on camera for the world to see. Like the little rich girl who wrote a diary complaining of how her comfortable life had been disrupted, how she wished the nation would come back to its senses. They published it all over the world. And then they arranged for all the appropriate visas and took her and her prosperous family out of the country. I thought about the other children in the streets. The ones whose mothers and fathers had been killed. What diaries they could have written, if only they had known how to read and write properly. But then I wonder if they would have written anything; they were too busy playing soccer in the huge ballroom of the Europa Hotel. It had been turned into a shelter for homeless kids—the Sarajevo soccer field had been turned into a cemetery.

It was the real people who managed to keep the city alive, the people wearing shoes with worn-out soles. When the war first broke out, I hated them for being so determined. But the more of them I killed, the more I began seeing them as men and women who were already condemned and in no need of my hatred. It was like counting bodies that were already laid out in a morgue.

I had no illusions about what they would offer someone like me when the war was over. It wouldn't surprise me if they rounded up us snipers and made us scapegoats to draw attention away from the leaders. They would probably execute us for crimes against humanity while the men who issued our orders ran for election in coalition governments or went off into comfortable exile.

I had no hope for the future, nor any great personal interest in the people who wandered into the sights of my rifle. Any attention I paid them was a passing professional interest. Not much more than the kind your doctor shows you until he abruptly turns his attention to his next appointment. I had developed the personality of a specialist. Everything I did was automatic.

One day, however, something strange happened on the road below my window.

I'd just shot four idiots who had tried to run across in broad daylight while shouting brash encouragement to each other. A crowd formed on the far side of the barricade. All of a sudden an old woman emerged from the crowd. She walked through a gap in the barricade and came out on the road. She must have been about eighty years old. I watched her through my telescopic sight, wondering what she was up to. She had a shopping bag with her. She walked past the four bodies and entered our side of the forbidden zone. I let her make it to our side just to see what she would do. She sat down on a block of concrete and rested for a few minutes. Then she got up and walked back over to her side, took a few minutes of rest again, and made the same dangerous crossing over to our side.

She could have kept on going and broken out of the besieged section, but she turned and went back to her point of origin. She made about half a dozen crossings that took up the entire afternoon, and then disappeared back into her side of town.

I was spellbound. She seemed totally oblivious of the danger. She was like a little toddler who walks out onto a four lane highway not understanding what she's doing. It threw me off badly. What was she trying to do? What did she have in that plastic shopping bag that she dragged along with her?

She was back again the next day. She sat on her side of the forbidden zone and fumbled in her shopping bag. She took out what seemed to be a photograph. She pulled it close to her face and peered into it. I saw her lips begin to move. I turned the scope of my rifle on full magnification. She was talking to whoever was in the photograph. At some point she smiled at the image lovingly and kept repeating endearments. Then a pitiful look came over her and she began weeping, all the while muttering to the photograph. She put the photo back in her bag, stood up wearily, and headed across the vacant road. She walked lumberingly, her kerchief-covered head bobbing from side to side, keeping time to the slow progress of her bowed legs. Completing her journey over to our side, she sat down to rest. She took out the photograph again and glanced at it, as if using it to gather strength for the return journey. A few minutes later, she waddled back to her side of town and disappeared behind the barricade.

I lay in my bed, tossing and turning all night. It was the first time someone in the forbidden zone had been in the sights of my rifle without my firing a shot. What was she doing crossing back and forth like that? Was she out of her mind? Was she senile? Why hadn't someone stopped her from walking out into nowhere?

Her talking like that to the photo sent my mind travelling back to my grandmother's house. I felt as if I were twelve again and sitting next to my grandmother out on the porch of her house. She had this same habit. She would sit and talk to a photo of one of her sons for hours on end. One day, the dike behind the house broke and water flooded the basement of the house. She whispered a blow-by-blow account of the incident to the photo of her son while hitting her knees in distress. My mother said it was foolish to talk to photos. But my grandmother chided her, telling her that a photo captured a person's soul, that if you talked to a person's picture you automatically talked to the person himself. She claimed that she sometimes heard her son answer her while she talked to him like that, and, imagine, he lived over two hundred miles away. I didn't care one way or the other. I never had much patience for riddles.

But this old Babushka haunted me for most of the night. I hoped that she would disappear and that the whole thing would go no further. Just before dawn I fell into a deep sleep.

Later, I ate some cheese for breakfast and made myself some tea. Usually I went straight to my lookout to check things out before breakfast. But that morning I think I was trying to delay taking up position, for fear of seeing her there again. I took my time drinking the tea, then moved behind my rifle and peered through the scope. I sighed with relief; there was no one around.

But half an hour later, her plump shape appeared from behind the barricade. I cursed under my breath. She was bringing her ancient presence into my space to ruin the simplicity of my life. I had done this my way for months, and done it well. Now I had to break stride and take her into account.

I didn't want to think of her as a person, but my mind went its own way. Who was she? Did she have a family? Where did she live? Was the person in the photo still alive? Who was the person in the photo, anyway? And how could I possibly shoot an old woman who walked back to her side of town as soon as she had made it to our side? I had always been a strict gatekeeper, but she wasn't showing any desire to break through.

A man in his forties or fifties might have found such absurdity amusing. But I couldn't understand any of it. I thought of calling my commander to ask him what he thought of all this. But I didn't want to let on that she had me muddled. So I decided to wait and see for myself.

Reaching the midpoint of the road, she stopped and raised a hand to shield her eyes from the sun. She looked straight in my direction. She stood there peering at my window as if she knew I was there! I saw her face through the scope. Her eyes were looking straight into mine. I was sure of it. A hundred ancient lines were etched across her face. I could swear she knew that our eyes had locked. She stood there staring for what seemed like an eternity, and then turned and walked back to her side of town.

I found sleep altogether impossible that night. I tried to blank her out of my mind, but I couldn't stop seeing her staring at my window. At one point, tossing and turning in bed, I even wondered if the other side hadn't sent her there on purpose, just to make me lose my nerve.

I was drinking some tea the next morning when I suddenly sensed her presence on the road. I hurried to the rifle and peered through the scope. She was there again, like a curse that follows you no matter how many prayers you recite. This time she seemed to be walking with new purpose. Arriving at the midpoint, she stopped, shielded her eyes from the sun, and stared up in my direction again. Then she bent down and pulled a cardboard sign from her bag. She held the sign up. Written in big block letters in our language was one word: "PLEASE."

I broke out into a terrible sweat, my stomach churning. I dropped to the floor and crouched there, holding onto my belly. I felt like an executioner whose hood had suddenly been torn off. I was afraid to get up and look, and stayed on the floor for over an hour. Then, gathering all my nerve, I stood up slowly and peeked through the scope. She was nowhere in sight.

That night, the word "PLEASE" kept flashing in my mind. I tried to scan the strip of forbidden territory using my infrared sensor, but my eyes were useless. An entire convoy could have driven across the boulevard and I wouldn't have noticed a thing. She was all I could think of. She wasn't an anonymous Babushka anymore. She made me think of my mother, my grandmother, and every mother that had come before them. She was a harrowing reminder of the people we had been before everything had gone insane. Was it any wonder she stood in the middle of the forbidden zone talking to a photograph? For all I knew, her family might have abandoned her and left her to fend for herself in this city where almost anything edible had to pass through a pitiless black market.

I prayed that she would not appear again. The message she had flashed from four floors down was beyond my understanding. "PLEASE," it said. But please what? Please stop shooting our young? Please stop the war? Please be nice to the United Nations? Please let the food convoys through? Please lower the price of cabbage? Please what?

Eleven in the morning. Dear God, again she appeared, kerchief over her head, trailing the same shopping bag. She walked over to the midpoint and stood still. It was a cloudy day. She stood there looking up, staring straight at me. And then she reached into her bag and brought out the photograph again. She glanced at it, closed her eyes, and hugged it to her bosom. A few moments later, she put the photo back in her shopping bag. From the bag she now extracted a cardboard sign that was nearly twice as large as the first one. I peered through the scope, squinting to read the writing. When I saw the message my heart pounded loudly a few times, and then it seemed to stop altogether.

The sign read: "PLEASE DO IT NOW. IT IS ENOUGH."

Holding the sign up, she slipped the kerchief off her head and stood there bareheaded, hair white as snow. She had a crucifix in her hand and she crossed herself with it and pressed it to her bosom. And all this time I hadn't even wondered if she were Catholic, Orthodox, or Muslim. Her age and bearing had been all that mattered.

A silent scream shattered my mind. I think if I had opened my mouth the whole of Sarajevo would have stood still. I felt like an infant forced into a world he wanted no part of. The gates I had shut tight in order to stay blind to what I had become blew apart. I had become immune to people begging for their lives, scurrying around like rats trying to find a safe hole. It was almost embarrassing to see them value their misery so much to want to keep it alive. But this old woman wasn't begging me to spare her so she could go on struggling with life. She was begging me to release her from it.

I looked through the scope again, my whole body trembling. I imagined pulling the trigger and saw how her tired legs would buckle without complaint, how her eyes would close for one final prayer. But I was an executioner, not a mercy killer. She was pleading for something which the others did everything to avoid. It turned me inside out.

And then it was as if I saw her entire life flash before my eyes. I saw her in labour giving birth to our mothers and fathers. I saw this Babushka, not very educated, but wise in the important things, going about her daily business without complaint, as long as it taught her children the meaning of simple survival. She cut a heroic figure next to our generals and presidents. Watching her standing in the square, her hand clutching her crucifix to her bosom, it dawned on me that the rest of us were clowns. She was what was left of our conscience, the witness of our cursed history.

She stood determined in the forbidden zone. She held the sign up and waved it slightly, like a beggar waving an empty cup. Her innocence awakened a long lost indignation in me. Her pitiful old age reminded me of the past and everything decent that we had lost in our hunger for revenge and retribution. Our warlords suddenly seemed like wastrels who had scorched our lives for a pittance.

I didn't cry when my mother died, nor when my father didn't return from the war. I hardened myself, thinking it would help me to survive the surrounding insanity. But now, this old woman—with legs bent from years of walking down streets corrupted by violence—burst the barricades of my heart. The rifle scope misted over and I couldn't see through it anymore. I left the rifle and hurried into the front room and went straight to the window. I stuck my head out, mindless of the sniper from the other side who might easily have shot me. I shouted to her: "Babushka! No, Babushka! Babushka! Please! I can't do such a thing."

She did not respond. She stood her ground. It felt as if an elderly grandmother was asking me to bring her a stool for her tired legs and I was refusing. I couldn't bear it any longer. I ran down the four flights of stairs, out the building and into the zone, surprised that no one from the other side took a shot at me. Perhaps they too were looking at the same scene trying to make sense of it.

I ran up to her and gathered her in my arms and mumbled comforting words to her that I never thought I would ever be able to say to anyone. I cradled her head and told her that all would be well in the end. But she shook her head and kept repeating the same word: "Please."

A crowd had formed around the gap in the barricade and was watching the whole thing in silence. They knew I was the enemy, but they made no move to attack me. The old woman turned her face up to mine. She smiled with a tired knowingness that promised nothing could change her mind. I fell into her blue eyes. They stretched decades back, with no judgment in them. Just a tired beseeching look that begged me to comply.

I bent down my head, lifted her hand, and kissed it gently. And then, unable to look her in the face any longer, I turned around quickly and walked back with wooden legs and stumbled into the apartment in a state of shame and stupor.

I hurried to the rifle and looked through the scope. Damn it, she was still there. I couldn't get the expression in her eyes out of my mind. It wasn't the expression of one who was tired of looking after herself. No, her eyes looked like the eyes of one who was tired of seeing what was happening around her. Perhaps it was too late, perhaps we had taken our brashness too far. Maybe our grandmothers and grandfathers were sick and tired of us now and preferred that we write our own history and sign our own names to it.

She was still standing exactly where I'd left her. Her lips were moving almost imperceptibly. Her right hand still clutched the crucifix to her bosom. Watching her through the scope, I saw that the crowd had edged through the gap in the barricade and was standing in plain view on the side of the road. It resembled a respectful group arriving at the funeral of a dignitary.

I heard in my mind the irritating voices of our leaders giving

their self-righteous speeches, promising to seek vengeance on behalf of our grandparents. Their words were empty useless lies. This
Babushka who stood below, bareheaded, bowlegged, had seen
their vengeance and wanted no part of it anymore.

She was tearing at my heart. I realized that I, Radic, the son of
an honest man, would be lost for the rest of my days if I didn't find
some way to reclaim my honour.

My eyes remained filled with tears, blurring my view. I in-
creased the magnification of my viewfinder to move in closer and
see better. The crucifix in her hand filled the viewfinder. And
then suddenly out of nowhere, an image of the Christ filled my
mind. I hadn't thought of him since the day the priest recited the
prayers at my mother's funeral. Now, I saw him stretched out on
the cross. One of his arms was nailed to the wooden crossbeam.
But the nail in his other arm had come loose and he was hanging
there in great pain. I was at the foot of the cross, staring up at his
suffering, weeping.

He looked down at me and there was love and pity in his eyes.
Struggling to get the words out, he begged me to drive the loose
nail back into his hand so that his end would be quicker. I shook
my head and mumbled that I couldn't do such a thing. But he
smiled at me sadly, and asked me to trust his wisdom and do as he
asked. And my sleeping heart was awakened by his pain. I found a
rock and a nail at the foot of the cross and climbed up to the crossbeam. Reaching him, I kissed the palm of his hand, set it in place,
and positioned the nail. I lowered my head, begged his blessing,
and then lifting my head and focusing my eyes, I used everything
that I had learned in all those horrible senseless months to drive
the nail in, quickly and accurately.

Down on the road, a few men emerged from the crowd and approached the old woman. They lifted her lifeless body and began
carrying her behind the barricade. One enemy soldier stayed behind for a moment. He glanced up in my direction, waved at me
sadly, then turned and followed the others.

I grabbed my rifle, stumbled into the front room, and threw it out the window just as I had the medal. Then my eyes were drawn to the Miljaka River and the sculpture of the bicyclist. It was still hanging there in midair on a cable stretching across the darkening sky of Sarajevo.

Kigali, Imana

I met him in a shopping mall in Montreal. Even though it was just the beginning of summer, we were already in the third day of a cruel heat wave. It was ninety-eight degrees at eleven-thirty in the morning. I was in the shopping mall on the pretext of buying some summer shirts, but it was the central air conditioning that had drawn me there.

I was sitting on the ledge of a fountain admiring the goldfish when I felt his presence next to me. He was standing very still, his eyes fixed on the water rushing out of the fountainhead. He stood with his arms hanging by his sides, palms out, head raised a little, as if he were looking at a point on some faraway horizon.

He wore a white shirt, a pair of perfectly pressed trousers, and immaculately shined shoes. He seemed so lost in his thoughts that it surprised me when he suddenly turned to me and said, "The water is good, is it not?"

"On a day like today, even a photograph of a waterfall would be a relief," I answered, smiling courteously, wanting him to know that I didn't mind him talking to me.

His attention returned to the fountain. Then a few moments later, he turned to me again and said, "I was just now remembering a waterfall I knew. It was a giant, wonderful waterfall. We would swim in its waters and dip our heads under its powerful current. The rushing water stopped all thought. It was a magnificent waterfall."

But his look of contented reminiscence evaporated suddenly. The corners of his mouth turned down, as if clamping on some pain that was on the verge of erupting. His eyes were no longer filled with courtesy. They were the eyes of a wounded doe.

"Memories of my homeland are not as pleasant as a waterfall," he said, pausing to observe my reaction, as if waiting to see if I would permit him to tell more. I knew that hesitant look. I had seen it before on the faces of people I had met while travelling, just moments before they revealed something that they couldn't keep silent any longer.

I tried to leave him an opening in case he needed one: "You seem to have experienced something ... " I let my voice trail off, leaving him to own the sentence and complete it.

His gaze fell on two teenagers who were walking by, carrying large shopping bags and giggling with one another. Watching them head towards the exit of the mall, he said, "Where I come from, people walking like this, shopping in a cool place, not afraid of never making it back home ... it's nothing but an impossible dream."

"Where are you from?" I asked.

He hesitated for an instant and answered, "It might make you uncomfortable to know."

"I don't see why."

"Well, you have seen the worst of us on your television. I do not come from a good place." He stopped abruptly, as if he had said more than he intended. He turned around and walked away without another word.

Realizing that he wasn't about to return, I stood up and hurried after him. He stopped at a newsstand and began looking at the newspapers. I caught up with him, positioned myself next to him, and pretended to look at some magazines. He noticed me out of the corner of his eye, but didn't say anything and continued scanning the newspapers. A copy of *Time* magazine caught my eye. It was one of the most striking covers ever published by the editors of *Time*. There was a sombre photograph of two children, a closeup of their heads. The two children looked tortured beyond repair. They weren't starving like the children in Somalia; their eyes were filled with a harrowing emptiness, the kind that moves in to numb body and soul after some sudden mind-blowing horror. There was a headline printed across the photo, mercifully drawing attention away from the stricken faces. It read: "If there are devils in hell, then hell must be empty, for the devils are all in Rwanda."

I picked up the copy of *Time* and paid for it. I was staring at the disturbing cover when he said, "I told you I do not come from a good place."

Not wanting to embarrass him, I quickly tucked the magazine into my bag. We began walking through the mall together, covering our uneasiness by looking into the showcases, commenting occasionally on some of the electronic gadgets on display.

We arrived at the fast food stalls and sat at a table in the common seating area. He glanced at the neon-lit photos of the food. I wanted to ask him if he was hungry, but I hesitated. I didn't know if he had any money on him. His clothes were immaculate and his shoes were shining. But that didn't say anything about how much money he had in his pockets. I had seen many refugees arrive in the country penniless, but dressed proudly.

"Why don't we have lunch together?" I suggested.

"My wife and I have been on your government's generous refugee programme since we arrived two weeks ago. I must watch my expenses till we get settled. So I ate at home before coming out. But please, you go ahead. It must be time for your lunch," he answered.

Not certain whether he had really eaten or not, I suggested, "Then I'll buy us both a snack."

He rose abruptly from his seat. "No, no, please. I'm not hungry. I ate at home already." He sat back down, satisfied that the point was settled.

I had lived in Africa and knew that he might feel offended if I insisted any further. I excused myself and walked over to one of the food counters. I picked up a can of soda pop, then changed my mind and asked for a cup of tea.

Arriving back at the table, I saw that he had lit a cigarette and was holding it between his thumb and forefinger, puffing on it, lost in thought. It reminded me of the way African village elders held their cigarettes when they sat in deep conversation with one another.

He came out of his reverie with a polite smile. "May I see the magazine you bought?" he asked.

I hesitated, then pulled the magazine out of my bag and handed it to him. He laid it on the table and stared at the cover for a moment. His gaze was so intense that the moment seemed to last much longer than it did. I shifted uneasily. He opened the magazine and thumbed through it until he arrived at the cover story.

I looked at the upside down page, wondering what he was seeing. There was a picture of a man and two women who had fallen against a storefront. Their eyes were shut. It seemed as if they were sitting on the sidewalk leaning their backs on the storefront. If it weren't for the blood on their clothes and the blood flowing around their bodies, they could just as well have been taking an afternoon nap.

He stared at the pictures dispassionately. "You know, this must look horrible to someone who has never set foot in Rwanda. But these pictures are tame. They do not reveal the real faces of the devils." He gave me back the magazine. I put it in my bag, wondering what he had witnessed in Rwanda to eclipse these shocking photos.

"My wife and I arrived here two weeks ago," he said. "Yet, it feels as if I were still in Kigali. Every night, my wife insists that we push the dining table against the door of the apartment. She says the noise of the table moving will awaken us should someone suddenly arrive in the middle of the night." I nodded. I had been in three wars as a civilian. I knew how long it took for the aftershocks to subside.

"Of course there's no need for the table. There's no one coming through the door. And even if anyone did come, I'd know it. I'm still the way I was in Kigali. At night, I close my eyes, but my mind stays awake and listens carefully. It has become a habit, like shaving." He began to smile, but the tension around his mouth reined in the smile and turned it into a grimace.

"Were you raised in Kigali?" I asked.

"Yes. I grew up in Kigali. I won a scholarship when I was seventeen and went to university in Indiana to study English literature. A strange choice perhaps, not as practical as economics or engineering. I received my Master's degree and was hired by the government of Rwanda. I became a senior official in Kigali, analyzing and designing educational projects."

His attention wandered to some people sitting at another table.

Then, suddenly, without any warning, he turned his eyes abruptly into mine and declared, "I am a Hutu."

We sank into silence.

He had just admitted to being a member of a tribe that had, in the span of a few weeks, decimated a few hundred thousand members of a rival tribe. This much I had gathered from the news reports on TV, but the sound bites had been short and incomplete. So I had done my own research and pieced together the larger story about Rwanda. I found out that the Tutsi, although no more than fourteen percent of the population, had managed to dominate the Hutu majority ever since the fifteenth century. Long before any foreign power had arrived in the country, the Tutsi had succeeded in ruling the Hutu through a despotic monarchy. And to aggravate matters more, the Tutsi had been a pastoral people. They had done well managing their herds, while the Hutu had followed a less profitable agricultural life. So the potential for animosity between the two tribes was an ancient one.

And that animosity worsened when the Belgians moved in as a result of the League of Nations agreement. The Belgians governed Rwanda using the established Tutsi monarchy. They awarded the Tutsi special favours and positions. For some reason best known to themselves, the Belgians considered the Tutsi more intelligent than the Hutu, since they were taller, had a slightly fairer skin colour, and were more prosperous. They issued identity cards, identifying each person as *Hutu, Tutsi,* or *Other.* The cards helped the Belgians establish an apartheid system that perpetuated the old myth of Tutsi superiority. As for the Tutsi elite they had no difficulty agreeing with the Belgians' prejudicial evaluation and took to ruling the Hutu with renewed self-confidence.

Years later, however, when the Belgians decided that it was time to give Rwanda back its sovereignty, they were faced with a rebellious Hutu majority. So they made an about-face, put the country into the hands of the Hutu majority, and left the Tutsi to their mercy. Large numbers of Tutsi were suddenly forced to flee to neighbouring Burundi.

In the years that followed, the exiled Tutsi formed a rebel army and fought the Hutu government forces in Rwanda with remarkable effectiveness. They called themselves the R.P.F. (Rwandese Patriotic Front) and demanded an end to the exclusion of Tutsi from the Rwandan government. Extremists in the Rwandan government called the R.P.F. *inyenzi* ("cockroaches"). And they called any Hutu who did not oppose the R.P.F. *ibyitso* ("accomplices"). When the Hutu President Juvénal Habyarimana signed a power-sharing peace pact with R.P.F., the extremists accused the President himself of being an *ibyitso*.

And then on the evening of April 6, 1994, the plane carrying the Hutu president was shot down over Kigali. There were no survivors. Some said that it was the president's own national guard that fired the rocket that shattered Habyarimana's plane. The Hutu extremists said that it was the doing of the Tutsi rebels.

The devils that escaped from hell—as *Time* put it—arrived in Rwanda a couple of hours after the president's assassination. They whispered in the ears of the presidential guard and it paid heed and coursed through Rwanda killing Tutsi civilians at random. And then more devils arrived and spread into the civilian population. Gangs of Hutu men, armed with sharp machetes, went on wild killing sprees, drunk on cheap liquor and dressed in bizarre colourful fashions looted from stores. One TV report showed them dressed in carnivalesque clothes, brandishing automatic rifles and machetes while happily waving at the cameras.

So when he told me that he was a Hutu, I felt a nauseating shiver. I forgot that I was in a shopping mall in North America. Frankly, I felt like bolting.

"Does it frighten you to be sitting at the same table with a Hutu?" he asked.

"Well, not all Hutu were killing," I answered, hoping I wasn't mistaken. He didn't confirm or contradict what I said.

"My name is Cyprien," he said. I gave him my own name and we stretched our arms across the table and shook hands. Taking his hand in mine, I couldn't help wondering whether it had hurt or killed anyone.

He turned the conversation away from himself and asked what I did for a living. I told him I was a writer. He nodded and said, "Yes, maybe that's why I feel at ease talking to you. Writers are good listeners, are they not?"

"Some listen. Some others are too busy writing," I answered.

I sensed that he was about to begin the main body of his story. For a moment I felt reluctant to listen. I suspected that what he was about to tell me might leave me shaken. I had already spent a year working on a story about Somalia. I wasn't sure if I was ready for more tragedy. But I let him continue and didn't interrupt him or ask any questions until he had finished. At one point, arriving at the worst part of it, he stopped and looked into my eyes. For a moment he seemed to be going to break down in tears. But he bit his lip and continued:

*

I am a Hutu, yes. But I married a Tutsi. My wife grew up a few houses away from my family's home. We knew each other practically all our lives, went to the same school together, played in the same places. By the time we were twelve we already knew that we would be married. Mind you, it wasn't at all an arranged marriage. We loved each other as children and we continued loving each other as grown-ups. My father died when I was fourteen, and my mother—although she didn't live to see the wedding—gave me her blessing before she passed away. My wife and I both had exceptional families. It's rare for a Hutu and Tutsi to marry, you know. We married in Kigali, two months after I returned from university in America.

Yesterday my wife threw a dish at the wall and said she wished that she'd never met me. And it has been only a year and a half that we've been married. I took her in my arms to comfort her and she fell right to sleep. Ever since we left Kigali she explodes like that and then falls asleep immediately after, remembering none of it when she wakes up. If it happens in the evening before she's had a chance to push the table in front of the door, I push it there myself, so that she'll see it in place if she wakes up in the middle of the night.

Last night after she fell asleep, I went out on the balcony to look at the stars, but there was too much light and smog. So I closed my eyes and remembered the stars back in Rwanda. I liked to climb onto the roof of our house in Kigali, lie on my back, and gaze up into the sky. Even in Indiana, where everything was American and always changing, I would find a quiet corner on campus, lie on the grass, and look up at the stars. They seemed to be the only things that remained constant. It comforted me to think that these same stars had been seen only hours ago by my own people. They were my link back to my family, a little like a cosmic fax system.

Kigali isn't as large as this city. Here you can walk out of your apartment and be anonymous in a few moments. A short walk and no one knows you. But in Kigali there's no such thing as easy anonymity. People can know which tribe you belong to just by looking at your features. You may not know this, but the Tutsi are generally taller than the Hutu, sometimes a little fairer.

It doesn't take long for word to travel from one end of Kigali to the other. On that fateful evening, just an hour after the president's plane exploded in mid-flight, whispering and grumbling spread through the town like an ominous wind ushering in a dark storm. I was having a late meeting in my office with two Belgians who had flown in from Brussels to discuss exchanging teachers with our ministry of education. When my secretary called me with news of the president's assassination, one of the Belgians turned pale and said in a hoarse voice, "This is the beginning of something that none of us will ever forget." The Belgians stood up, excused themselves, and hurried back to their embassy.

I hurried home to tune in the B.B.C. and listen to the news from London. I didn't trust our own radio stations to tell the truth. My wife was there with her mother, father and sister. My in-laws had sold their house and moved in with us. But I wasn't worried about our fate if violence broke out. I was sure we would be all right if we kept to ourselves.

The B.B.C. broadcast said that everything was confused in Kigali, that no one knew who was responsible for the president's death. Some bomb experts from Belgium were on their way to Kigali to examine the plane's wreckage. I myself didn't care who the assassins were. I had no quarrel with the Tutsi ... I was married to one. I tuned in one of our own radio stations. It was strange. The station always went off the air at ten o'clock. But this night, after the news, it remained on the air and broadcast music all night.

I had three foreign friends whom I had met through my work with the ministry of education. We had a good friendship, it was like having a lifeline back to my days in the West. One was an Italian nurse, another a teacher from France, and the third an engineer from Belgium. All three were competent professionals who had dedicated themselves to helping Rwanda. The French teacher had recently adopted a thirteen-year-old Tutsi boy. The papers had been signed and the boy was living with her.

I decided to visit them to see if they had any reliable news from their embassies. My friends lived in an apartment building reserved for foreign nationals. So I was surprised to see a dozen or so Tutsi huddled inside the courtyard of the building. I asked them what they were doing there. One of them explained that they felt safer being in the shadow of a building reserved for foreigners.

I told my friends about the group huddled downstairs. They said they had heard rumours about some killing in one part of town.

Someone from the Belgian embassy had called them to warn them that the military and youth militias had set up roadblocks throughout Kigali.

"Then why don't we hear the sounds of gunfire?" I asked.

"Because they're using machetes," answered my Belgian friend. I felt embarrassed to hear that my people had stepped back five hundred years.

We fell into silence. Their faces were drawn tight with worry. It's not easy to be a foreigner in a strange land. But being a foreigner in a land that's sinking into civil war is the worst. You never know which side may suddenly find you offensive and blame you for its predicament. You're no longer considered a benevolent stranger. You're seen as an impediment, or even worse, an unwanted witness.

Walking home that night, I took a deep breath of the night air. I was hoping it would relax me and clear my head. But I realized sadly that the Spring night air, which I had always loved, did not feel kind anymore. I no longer felt that this was my home. It reminded me of when I went to New York City on a Thanksgiving weekend while I was studying in Indiana. I got off at a wrong stop on the New York subway and found myself in a dangerous neighbourhood where even the sidewalks seemed to be trembling with tension. Here and there were characters lounging in doorways, looking as if one wrong word from you and they'd be at you. Walking through the streets of Kigali now, I checked every alleyway I passed, praying they would be empty. I heard gunfire in the distance.

When I arrived home, I found my father-in-law still awake. He whispered to me to tell him what I had heard and seen. He and I had never kept any secrets from one another. He had always been like a decent father to me. I had to treat him with respect and tell him the truth. After listening to my report he slumped into a chair and stared out the window.

I didn't sleep that night. I sat huddled next to the radio, listening to the news. The B.B.C. reported that the situation was getting worse by the hour. The armed troops weren't killing people only in the streets; they had begun forcing their way into houses and massacring the inhabitants.

I waited for the cover of dark the next day to make my way back to where my European friends lived. My wife and her family advised against going out into the streets. I came very near to saying that I was a Hutu and didn't have much to fear. But I bit my tongue in time, grabbed my jacket, and walked out of the house, promising them that I'd be all right.

My friends were gathered in the apartment of the French teacher. My Belgian friend was beside himself with worry: "It's awful. Really awful. We just heard from the embassy. It's ten times worse than we imagined. This isn't a civil war. It's a genocide. Many of the roads are blocked. The Hutu are searching for any Tutsi trying to leave the country. They're killing them wherever they find them … and they're even killing Hutus who won't denounce their Tutsi neighbours. Age makes no difference. Babies, my God, adults, children, all, *mon Dieu*. Thousands have spilled over into neighbouring Burundi, totally destitute. A town has formed near the border, without any services whatsoever. I know the place—it was barren land only a few weeks ago."

The French teacher was sitting on one of her packed suitcases looking grim. "I tried to leave this morning with my boy and a U.N. worker whom the embassy insisted I take along with me. We were stopped at a checkpoint. The man in the car ahead of us stuck his hand out the window, offering a lot of money. The guard at the checkpoint grabbed the money, shoved it in his pocket, and pulled the man out of his car. The poor man looked bewildered. The soldier put his revolver to the man's head and pulled the trigger. A woman screamed from inside the car; the soldier stuck his gun through the window and shot her too. The soldier then approached our car, stuck his head in, and stared at my boy. He ordered us to get out. He took my boy aside and told me I wasn't allowed to save a Tutsi. I quickly pulled my son's adoption papers out of my purse. But then I froze as he put his revolver to my son's head. The U.N. worker was very quick, God bless him. He shouted that I was an important diplomat, that the boy was my legal son and there would be all hell to pay if he were hurt. Another second and the soldier would have pulled the trigger. Now we're leaving with the Belgian convoy. There's no other way out of here."

She paused and looked at me with pity in her eyes. "Why are you looking at me that way?" I asked, irritated. Her voice faltered a little, "You have a Tutsi wife. What are you going to do, my friend?"

Her question jolted me. Until now, I had only worried about keeping my family safe from the crossfire between the Hutu and the Tutsi. I considered ourselves outside the conflict. As far as I was concerned, we were neither Hutu nor Tutsi. We were just a family. It hadn't really sunk in that I was a Hutu and that my wife was a Tutsi and that this union of ours had thrown us on the wrong side of both sides.

My friends left Kigali that afternoon. We exchanged reluctant goodbyes and they gave me their addresses in Europe and told me I would always have a place to stay if I needed one. I still have the paper with the addresses in my wallet.

You know, it's frightening to have foreigners leave your country because it's no longer safe. It's like being left behind on a sinking ship. My mind was full of questions. What would we do? Would the trouble spread to our own district? How would I manage to keep my wife and her family safe?

My in-laws were already asleep when I returned home. But my wife was waiting up for me. She pulled me into our room, shut the door, and asked me in a hushed voice to tell her what was happening in Kigali. I put my arms around her and told her that things might get a little difficult for us all. I told her it was because she and her family belonged to the wrong tribe. It wasn't easy to tell her this, but I had to be honest with her. She shook her head and said, "Yes, but you're a Hutu. And I'm your wife. They will not hurt us."

Half an hour later, just as we were falling sleep, we heard a horrible scream. I'm not the same man I was before that scream. Please, you must understand. You speak to me as if I were worthy of sitting here and speaking with you about shopping malls, lunches, and pretty fountains. But perhaps I am not. I wear a clean pressed shirt and I'm careful when I shine my shoes, but that does not change what I saw that night or during the days that followed.

I threw my trousers on and hurried out. The lights were on at a house just down the street. Some men were huddled at the front door. It was the house of our neighbourhood cobbler. I had spoken to him just a few days ago when he had repaired the soles of my shoes and done a very good job of it. I pushed through the crowd and what I saw made me wish I had been born blind. Lying in front of the door was the cobbler. His legs had been cut off just below the knees and a pair of shoes had been forced onto the stumps. His wife was bent over his body. She opened her mouth to scream again but no sound came from her. The men tried their best to make her let go of what was left of her husband, but her arms seemed to have a strength far more powerful than theirs.

I turned to one of the men and asked him who had committed this horror. He looked amazed at my question. Then, without any warning, he slapped my face and spat in my eye. "Your own people did this," he said, his mouth twisted with hatred.

A few weeks ago, this same man and I had drunk coffee together, but now he despised me as if I were the devil himself. The man standing next to him had a walking stick with him. He leaned forward belligerently and raised the stick over his head. I mumbled that I was very sorry about what had happened. I turned and hurried home, hoping that none of them would run after me.

I found my wife still standing where I had left her in the bedroom. She was pale and trembling. "Who have they killed?" she stammered. I lied to her. "The cobbler has died of a heart attack. That was his grieving widow screaming."

The militia was diabolically clever. It spilled enough blood in each neighbourhood to let the Hutu civilians have a whiff of it and get ideas of their own. The message went around that anyone could join in. All that was needed was a weapon. A broadcaster at a popular radio station founded by Hutu extremists broadcast a special message to the Tutsi, "You cockroaches know very well you are made of flesh. We won't let you kill us. We will kill you."

It took only a few hours for the terrible fever to spread. Men, some not older than sixteen, poured into the streets in gangs. Encouraged by their political and civil leaders, the youth militia, the *interahamwe,* meaning "those who attack together," helped spread the massacres from region to region. Neighbours hacked neighbours to death. Co-workers hacked one another to death in workplaces. Priests killed their parishioners. School teachers killed their students. Your street gangs in the West are polite diplomatic missions compared to what rushed onto the streets of Kigali. They broke into liquor and clothing stores. They got drunk and clothed themselves in ridiculous colourful outfits. Some of them took to wearing skirts and hats taken off the racks; some even painted their faces in strange colours. They raged through the streets all night long, persuading and coercing others to join them. As the band grew in size, the men armed themselves with sharpened machetes, spears, sticks, and rocks. It was as if they had broken into an armaments museum and brought out weapons dating from every historical period.

Early next morning, there was a cacophony of car horns in our street. I hurried my wife and her family down to the room in the basement and carried down whatever food and water I could find. I told them to stay there, remain perfectly quiet, and not come out for any reason. I reassured them that all would be well if we remained quietly in hiding. Then I ran back upstairs, parted the curtains, and peered out.

The Hutu militia, accompanied by hundreds of civilians, had flooded into the neighbourhood. Some were leaning out of car windows celebrating their new-found power over life, bottles of cheap liquor dangling from their hands. Others walked with dance-like movements, waving their weapons above their heads as if to keep rhythm with the swagger of their bodies. It was bewildering to watch their fierce lusty joy. The whole thing resembled a celebration at the close of a rich harvest.

A film director couldn't have done a better job of creating the scene of pandemonium that followed. Tutsi men, women, and children, startled by the car horns, made the error of running out into the streets to see what was happening. They were herded into the square at the end of the street and surrounded by Hutus armed with guns and machetes. Some of the men fired in the air. The shots made the Tutsi stampede. Children, separated from their parents, ran in all directions. Grown men brayed with fear, sensing the inevitability of their end. They ran around in circles, as if hoping that the dusty air would part and reveal a miraculous exit into another time and place. I saw women standing perfectly still, paralyzed with the shock of having lost their children and husbands, and others, screaming out names in wild desperation, voices hoarse with terror.

Then the wall of men armed with machetes closed on the crowd. I didn't want to watch, but something pushed me to look this thing in the face. It took no more than a few minutes. As the dirt and gravel of the road turned into a muddy dark red, the killers took to chanting—an unearthly and beastly sound. And then it was over. The men moved on, leaving the bodies heaped one over the other, like sugar sacks brought to market for auction.

Before sunset that day, they killed over ten thousand Tutsi in Kigali, thousands more in the rest of the country. Try to imagine it, my friend. Pretend for a moment that ten thousand were killed in this, your own city, in the span of a few hours. No earthquakes or floods or other nation invading with weapons of mass destruction, not even hand-to-hand combat. Just outright one-way slaughter. Think of what your streets would look like were this to happen here. No, you can't conceive it ... and maybe it speaks well for you that you can't.

There were no more foreigners in Kigali. Many had left reluctantly, worried about the Rwandan friends they were leaving behind. I felt alone now, abandoned in a place that no longer seemed like home. Even though I was a Hutu walking in streets that were under the absolute and terrifying power of my own people, I felt like a man walking through a holocaust, hoping that he wouldn't be spotted and carried off.

That afternoon I was forced to leave the house to buy some bread. Rounding a corner, I came face to face with a Hutu militia man. He stuck a machete in my hand and growled, "Make yourself useful." I stood on the road, stunned, the machete dangling from the same hand I had used to hold my university degree on the day of my graduation. I ran back home, forgetting that the machete was still dangling from my hand until I lifted my arm to open the front door.

My wife and her family were huddled in the basement. My wife cried out: "The entire city is screaming. We can hear it even down here. Don't lie to us. How bad is it?"

The screams in the distance were like an airborne plague of sound that hovered over the rooftops and haunted you no matter where you went. I couldn't endlessly minimize what was happening. I told them of the looting and the massacres and tried to sound reassuring by keeping my voice level, as if I were announcing a passing bout of bad weather.

My father-in-law asked me if they had begun going into any of the houses in our own district. I shook my head and promised again that we would all be safe because I was a Hutu. And, after all, I was a fairly senior government official, only a step or two away from being a deputy minister. I promised them that if we stayed quiet, the killers would leave our house alone. My father-in-law raised an eyebrow but I turned away, not wanting to reveal my own worry.

My wife made me swear not to go out into the streets again. I agreed, locked the door of the house and joined them in the basement. We had some porridge, bread, water, and a dozen sweet cakes. It was barely enough for a few days. We settled down to being prisoners in our own house, hoping that no one would draw attention to us by coming to our rescue.

Sitting in the windowless room in our basement, unwanted images forced themselves on my brain. I began wondering how these in-house executions were accomplished. First, a violent banging on the door, then surprised shouts, followed by the wet dull sounds of machete hacks ... and agonized wails followed by silence, until another house was entered and a new wave of pandemonium unleashed. I shuddered to think that this was what we were hiding from.

I found it ironic that I, a Hutu, had taken to feeling the same terror felt by the Tutsi. When I was younger and the political situation had been the reverse, I had felt the unease of being a Hutu. My best friend and I were walking down a street one evening coming home from a soccer game when a group of Tutsi boys stopped us and asked us to pay them the price of safe passage. Since we had no money on us, they spat on us and beat us senseless. Just as I was losing consciousness, I heard one of them say, "You're just a Hutu. You're just a peasant." I awoke in the hospital to see a surgeon sewing up my wound, but then he injected me with an anaesthetic and asked me to count backward to ten.

When we were released from the hospital, my friend and I took to training each other. We hit and spat on each other, called each other dirty names. After a couple of weeks, we became immune to the blows and insults and felt ready if ever they stopped us again. But they didn't.

Sequestered in the small room in the basement, I was no longer able to see what was happening on the streets. The radio was our only lifeline to the nightmare that had emerged to replace the Kigali I once knew and loved. It struck me that the local broadcasts reported the news as if they were reporting a legitimate war, as if the Hutu and Tutsi were foreign to one another, armed citizens of separate worlds.

There was a table in the room which we would sit around when we weren't stretched out on the straw mats on the floor. My mother-in-law knitted a lot. She would let out a deep sigh every time she reached the end of a few lines of knitting. Hearing her sigh, her daughters would glance at one another and say something comforting to her. The mother would respond by reminding them that she was old and didn't matter. She would say that what was important was the safety of the rest of us. And then she would sigh again and sink back into her sad thoughts. My father-in-law hardly said a word. One evening he ignored our protests, walked upstairs, and went to sleep in his own bed. He returned the next morning carrying a heavy scrapbook filled with old family pictures. He sat there staring at the pictures for hours on end, breathing very softly through parted lips.

I tuned in the B.B.C. world news service every morning, afternoon and night. One broadcast said that existing words weren't adequate, that new words would have to be invented to describe the horror. But there was no serious talk of sending in troops to confront the killers. Another broadcast said that the Americans were hesitant to come in because of the treatment they had received in Somalia. How many men had they lost there? How many had they readily given up in Vietnam and Kuwait? I found their sudden reticence unconvincing.

Everyday the B.B.C. reported that corpses were being heaped on the sidewalks. Men, women, and children were falling everywhere, hacked and pierced by sharp steel. I would listen to the reports and wonder how the world could know of such a methodical and total massacre without feeling compelled to intervene. They had come into our territory years before when the mining and the harvests were good. If they did not come now, was it because we had little left to offer, only our gratitude?

Our supply of food was dwindling. My father-in-law had stopped eating, claiming that he no longer had any appetite. We tried to talk him out of his fast, but he dismissed us with an impatient wave of the hand. My sister-in-law was only fourteen. It was a special hardship for her to be quarantined, cut off from her school friends. There was only one magazine in the room and she flipped through it endlessly, not really concentrating on any of the pictures or text.

You must understand that the rest of what happened I must try and say in a cold and factual way. Otherwise I would not be able to say it. I remember reading a book by the French-Algerian novelist Albert Camus. It was called *The Outsider*. Maybe you have read it or heard of it. It amazed me how, in the beginning of the book, the narrator says: "Mother died today. Or, maybe, yesterday; I can't be sure." It was such a cold and detached thing to say. But consider what he must have gone through to come to a point where he could recount such an important event without feeling it, remaining only dimly aware of the fact that it had happened.

Anyway, it was early afternoon. We were still huddled in the basement. Suddenly we heard the sound of a jeep's engine and then its rude brakes. Next came a very loud knock on the door, as if made with the butt of a gun. There was more banging ... urgent, rude, insistent.

I thought over our situation quickly. It would be better to answer the door and speak with them, I concluded. After all, I was a Hutu. Why should I have remained in hiding? Did not my being a Hutu and holding a senior position in the government give me the privilege of keeping my wife and her family safe, regardless of their origins?

"Don't go up. We mustn't answer the door," pleaded my wife.

"We have to answer," I argued. "It's better if we behave normally. I'm a Hutu. If I don't answer the door, they'll take it as some admission of guilt." I took her by the hand and we edged up the stairs together.

I took a deep breath and opened the door to three soldiers, each with an automatic rifle as well as a machete slung over his shoulder. One wore the stripes of a captain, the other two were corporals.

The captain took a step forward. "You are Cyprien?" he asked, not using my last name.

"Yes, I am," I answered, doing my best to appear confident of my rights.

"Let me see your papers," he ordered.

I took my identity card from my pocket and handed it to him. It had my picture and stated that I was a Hutu. I also handed him my official government I.D., hoping it would have the power to send him on his way. He glanced at the papers carelessly, as if he already knew everything there was to be known about me. He handed back the papers and barely looking at my wife addressed her contemptuously, "And your papers. Where are they? Get them." She went into the bedroom and came back with her identity card. He glanced at it quickly and then scanned her face for what seemed an eternity. I'm sure he would have known she was a Tutsi even if he hadn't seen it marked on paper.

He turned his attention back to me. There was blame in his eyes, the kind reserved for an incorrigible traitor. He smiled sardonically. "It is a very rare thing these days, a marriage between a Hutu and a Tutsi. Very rare. Yes, very rare!" His words felt like fists thrown at my face.

He then walked into our house taking firm confident strides, just as if he were the owner of the house and we the intruders. My wife and I followed him into the sitting room. The two other soldiers entered the house, too, and closed the front door behind them. The latch of the door fell into place, like the cocking of a trigger. His assistants stood motionless near the door, while he strutted around the room, inspecting this and that. He seemed in no hurry at all.

All of a sudden he turned to me and said, "This is a fine dilemma. You must surely be aware of my orders." I wondered what orders these could be in a country that was in shambles.

He continued: "You are a Hutu. I'm forced to consider this. Your wife is a Tutsi, which is ... well ... not good at all." I glanced over at my wife when he said this. She was trembling. I hurried to her, sat her down in a chair, and put my hand on her shoulder.

I wondered what he would do next. The fact that he was talking in hints and innuendoes gave me some hope. Perhaps he had come to frighten us a little and nothing more.

He took to shaking his head suddenly, like a strict schoolmaster confronting a pupil who's gone hopelessly wrong. Then, gathering all his might, he slammed his hand down on the table next to where my wife sat. She screamed and cringed in her chair, pulling her knees up under her chin, covering her head with her hands.

The veins in his temples were bulging as he shouted: "We're working sixteen hours a day to purge this land of these monsters … and you have gone and married one!"

Then he turned away and shuffled around the room as if nothing had happened. I held my breath, hoping he wouldn't find the door leading to the basement.

He stopped in front of a framed picture hanging just a few inches away from the basement door. It was a photo of my wife's mother and father. I moved quickly from where I was standing in order to distract him away from the picture, but he stayed focused on it. He took the picture off the wall, turned, and held it up, as if presenting a piece of damning evidence to a jury.

"And who are they?" he demanded.

"They are my wife's parents," I admitted, unable to think of a convincing lie. I expected him to ask their whereabouts. But he did nothing of the sort. He hung the picture back in its place, straightened the frame, and sat down in a chair without another word.

I turned to my wife and asked her to prepare the three of them some cold drinks. I hoped that, if we exhibited some normal friendly gesture, he might have a change of heart and see us as harmless people. My wife returned a couple of minutes later with a tray and three glasses of iced tea. Her hands were trembling. The only sound in the room was of tinkling ice. As she approached him, he got up from his chair like a perfect gentleman and took the tray from her hands. Then he hurled it, glasses and all, at the picture of my in-laws. My wife froze where she stood.

He approached me. His face betrayed a sharp angular hatred. "Sit down," he ordered. I obeyed him. He pulled up a chair and sat facing me, leaning forward until our knees were nearly touching.

"I was sent here for a purpose, you know," he said to me. "Don't think that you will be rid of me so easily. I can't just leave you here and move on. They will want a report. There's only one reason both of you are still alive. You are a Hutu and have a job with the government. If you were a cobbler, I wouldn't think twice about slitting both your throats. But I am instructed—"

The sound of a stifled cough broke loose from the basement. My wife and I made the mistake of glancing at each other in panic. Maybe if we hadn't he might have thought that the sound came from outside the house. He stopped in mid-sentence, cocked his head to one side, and motioned to the two soldiers. They moved through the house warily, checking every room. Finally one of them noticed the door leading down to the basement. He opened it and peered down the stairs. Then he and the other soldier began descending the stairs, holding their rifles ready. I heard the slow creaking of the stairs and then my sister-in-law's screams and the shuffling of feet hurrying back up the stairs. The soldiers reappeared, dragging my sister-in-law by the arm.

"There are two more down there. An older man and woman," reported one of the soldiers. My wife and her sister exchanged terrified glances.

The captain threw me a disgusted look and hurried down the stairs to see for himself. He came back up a few moments later. He sat back down in his chair, folded his arms, and stared at me with ominous gravity.

I couldn't stand his accusatory silence. "But they are my family!" I cried indignantly.

"They are Tutsi," he corrected icily. "I see no reason why they should be your family."

He stood up from the chair with a look of exaggerated weariness, as if he were about to start a task which he had put off as long as possible. He walked up to my sister-in-law, grabbed her by the hair and shoved her back down the stairs. Then he turned to my wife and ordered her to follow her sister downstairs. My heart sank as my wife shut the door behind her. I had this vision of him sending his soldiers down to finish them all.

He sat at the table and motioned for me to sit down with him. Then, much to my surprise, he ordered his assistants to go and wait outside the house. That set my mind at ease a little.

"We have a situation here," he said. "I want you to know that I'm doing everything possible to control my anger. Now, you're an intelligent man and you know what's happening in Kigali. When we go into a Tutsi house, we do what we have to do. Everything happens quickly. There are no discussions. But I have controlled my heart in your case, not because I want to, but because a certain government official who favours you instructed me to help you in any way I can. So I'm forced to stop and go against the natural flow of history, not because I wish you to keep what you call your family, but because it would look foolish if word spread that a Hutu stood against another Hutu to protect his Tutsi wife and her parents. These are not times for silly heroics."

He took out a pack of cigarettes and offered me one. Although I hadn't smoked in over five years, I accepted, glad for this small gesture of civility.

"There may be a way out of this," he said, lighting the cigarette for me. "Perhaps I can make you understand that it's time you stopped being a hero and started thinking of yourself. You have a good job and seem to be favoured by some who are in positions of power. Why ruin all this for people who are not of your own blood?" He spread his hands in a gesture of resignation, as if there were no more to be said.

Through my growing confusion, I struggled to focus on his words, not to lose the thread of his subtle meanings.

"Yes, it's important that you come to your senses. Think ... it has been over five hundred years. We never got along with these people. They're a small part of the population, but they have pushed the rest of us around for too long. If we don't end this now, they'll put an end to us someday. No, we can never let that happen. So you must save what's left now."

I couldn't understand what it was that he wanted me to save. I decided to test him. "What is it that you want me to do? Walk out of here, leave them behind, and pretend they never existed? Why don't you just go your way and leave us alone? Leave us to get by the way we have been. There's no harm in that." I said this in the tone of a hopeful beggar.

He shook his head and laughed, as if amazed that I had said

something very childish. "You've spent too many years in those expensive foreign universities. You've forgotten what this is all about. There can be no forgiveness ... no forgiveness at all. And I'm saying this without passion. Don't confuse me with those hooligans running around the streets wearing silly carnival clothes." Then, stiffening his back, he added, "I'm under military orders. Maybe if some of those hooligans had come here you could have bought them off with a case of cheap liquor. But this is a military matter. I'm in uniform and very sober."

I remained silent and stared down at the floor; I couldn't bear to meet his cold methodical gaze. His frightening self possession was so different from the mayhem on the streets.

Then he said it, slowly and firmly, "You must choose now ... you cannot delay much longer." He stared at me expectantly, as if giving me a moment to understand his meaning.

"Choose what?" I asked, looking up from the floor uneasily.

"Choose who is to be spared." He said it with exaggerated patience, as if he were explaining something quite evident to a halfwit.

"You mean ... you want me to choose ... between myself ... and my family?" I asked, breaking out into a sweat.

"No, no! Your own life is not in question here! I've already told you that you have friends in important places. You're not listening, man! No, you must choose which of *them* you want spared. I can let you choose one of them ... only one." He paused and then added in a quieter voice, "I don't think it will be a difficult choice to make."

He sounded so casual saying this. His breathing hadn't changed a bit, even though he had just authored a nightmare. He was anything but the image of the panting marauders reported in *Time* magazine.

"I can't make such a choice. How can I condemn my wife's family? I'm not God," I pleaded.

He smiled cruelly. "Perhaps you're right. Perhaps you should not decide for them." Then, looking suddenly inspired, he said, "Yes, why not? Let your wife decide. It is her family and it is her life. It's not your problem." He stood up decisively, as if it were all settled. He opened the door to the basement and called up my wife. He motioned for her to sit down.

He walked to the front door and opened it. My wife's face lit up for an instant. "I think the two of you have something to discuss. I will return later," he said. And without another word, he walked out of the house, leaving me with this horrible burden.

I rushed to the window to see what he was doing. He said something to one of his assistants, then climbed into the rear seat of the jeep, leaned his head back, and pulled his cap over his eyes.

My wife begged me to tell her what he had said while she was downstairs. I turned my eyes away from hers. How was I to announce his strict proposition? How was I to make her understand the choice he wanted her to make? And, having explained it to her, how could I encourage her to choose any life but her own? Yet, could I admit to her or myself that I would expect her willingly to condemn her own family?

I felt rage at his cold bloodedness. Had he burst in shooting his automatic rifle or hacking away with his machete, I might have found it possible someday to forgive him for being a raving lunatic. But the horror of it was that he knew what he was doing. He was in full possession of his senses, aware of the situation he was creating, maybe even enjoying it. I wondered if he hadn't sat down at his kitchen table and planned it all on paper before arriving. Perhaps he knew all the details of our lives, had possessed an exact head count long before he pulled up in his jeep. To think that this cunning man was turning me into a powerless child. Any other time my job with the ministry of education would have required him to respect my title, even speak to me with deference.

It hurt my heart to see how vulnerable my wife looked. It shamed me to know that he had guaranteed my life would be safe from all harm. I felt I had been given an unfair advantage over this woman whom I had always considered my equal. How was I to tell this old school friend that our playground had suddenly been separated into two and I been given the greener part of it?

I said it rapidly: "He says he can't leave us alone."

"What do you mean he can't leave us alone? What does he want to do with us?" she asked, eyes widening. I tried to tell her, but my mouth remained locked.

"Don't treat me like a child. Tell me exactly what he said," she insisted.

I took a deep breath and shut my eyes. "He says he will not harm me, but that only ... that only one of you can be spared, that ... that it is ... you who must choose."

She stared back at me as if I had spoken a language she had never heard before. And then the meaning of it hit her. She buried her face in her hands and wailed into them, throwing her head from side to side as if in a trance. I hurried over to her side and urged her to stop. I reminded her that her family was downstairs, that, hearing her crying, they would imagine that something horrible had happened. Understanding the meaning of what I said, she stuck her hand in her mouth, biting it in silence, throwing her head from side to side in crazed despair.

I hurried over to the window to see what he was doing. He still had his cap over his face. I moved over to the door of the basement, thinking that I should shout down a reassuring comment to the others. But I faltered and walked back to where my wife was sitting.

"There's no way out of here. He's still out there," I said.

Coming back to herself, she answered, "I can't choose which one of them will live. I know it certainly won't be me who lives through this." Her face was drenched in sweat.

I tried reasoning with her, but she cut me short. "It's easy for you to sit there with all your immunity and tell me to choose. Imagine what you're asking me to do! It's against everything I've been taught. I can't save my life and condemn my own flesh and blood!"

"But think," I pleaded. "Your parents are aged. Maybe he'll show some mercy for your sister. Maybe we can reason with him. You're young and we have a whole life ahead of us. What are we to do? What choice do any of us have?" I felt cheap saying this. But what else could I have said?

Her eyes flashed, "How can you think of our life together at a time like this? We may be young, but does that mean we're more valuable? Who am I to decide?"

"Listen to me. If it weren't for me, he would already have killed all of you. The only reason he's allowing you to live is because I'm a Hutu. He doesn't want word to get out that they killed the wife of a Hutu official. He's expecting you to agree to be spared in return for your family. I'm sure he'll accept nothing else. If you refuse, he may say the hell with it and kill us all. He doesn't care a bit about any of us."

She threw her head back in defiance and said, "Never!"

I walked to the window to look out again. He was out of the jeep and on his way back to the house.

He walked in and sat down at the table. He folded his arms, leaned back in the chair, and stared at us with raised eyebrows.

"Listen, you're asking the impossible," I pleaded. "There's no way that a daughter can choose to save herself and condemn the rest of her family. Think of what you're asking. Have you no God left?"

He leaped to his feet, face livid. "My God is Imana. I do not get involved with the Protestant and Catholic Gods. My God is the original force that ruled this land, long before the foreigners showed up, long before the Tutsi edged their way in and stole our land from us."

Imagine, he was using the name of Imana for his unholy purpose. Imana ... that's the word for God in our language. It means force of good and joy. "The Imana I know is a compassionate God," I countered.

"Compassion is irrelevant," he shot back. "This is about survival. First we allowed a minority to govern us for a very long time. And then we let in a foreign power that locked hands with them and ruled us through them. All we got were a few crumbs. But we were the majority. We had responsibility for this land from the day we arrived here. But tell me, what use is responsibility without power? So you see, it's out of the hands of gods now. It's in your own hands. And it's time you decided!" He paused and then addressed my wife in a mellow, reasonable voice, sounding very much like a wise loving elder, "I don't want to influence you. But I would imagine it would be logical for you to save one another. Is that not so? Don't you agree?"

His soothing tone of voice reminded me of a door-to-door vacuum salesman who once visited me in Indiana. The salesman had a smart way of presenting his vacuum cleaner. First, he would make a sales point, one that could not be argued against in any sane way. Then he would follow that up immediately by asking me, "Don't you agree? Is that not so?" He left me with no choice but to give a response that favoured his product—all this, without bothering to prove that I needed the product in the first place.

"This is a family affair," he continued. "You must decide. You must take responsibility now. You must choose to save yourself in order to keep the relationship with your husband intact. After all, the two of you can still have children. Your parents are old, and, as for your sister ... well, I admit, it's a hard choice. After all, I do have feelings too, but these are difficult times. In any case, it would be easier if you realized once and for all ... you and your husband need each other to survive. Do you understand?"

At the mention of the word *survive*, my wife shook her head in defiance. He stared at her rebellion with feigned surprise. "You mustn't torture yourself like this," he advised. Then, he abruptly changed his tone. "You have two minutes to decide. If you don't, I will make the decision for you and it will be a surprising and terrible one." His eyes glittered with menace.

All of a sudden, my wife spoke out with perfect lucidity. "There's no balance in this. You're offering us one life for three deaths. Where's the fair bargain?"

He didn't hesitate for a reply: "But I have really made it two for three ... don't forget that you get to keep your husband. I could have already shot him for treason."

My wife crumpled into silence. Then, a moment later, much to my surprise, she asked him, "How would it be done?" The man himself was slightly taken aback. But he regained his authoritative composure and answered, "You will leave the house. The rest will happen on its own. It will be very quick."

I would have bashed his head in with the butt of his own rifle. I would have wished on him what they did to the cobbler. Calm or not, he was a monster, a modern bureaucratic version of a stupid five-hundred-year-old quarrel.

He took to pacing the floor. I watched his dusty boots and wondered how many front doors they had kicked in, how many ribs they had smashed, how many lifeless bodies they had shoved aside to make way for his unholy swagger.

He turned to my wife. "Look. It's better you left without talking to them. Just take your clothes and walk out. You will be checked into a refugee camp that is under the protection of the United Nations. You will both be safe. You can come back when the fighting is over. Those are my orders. Everything has already been arranged." He said it as if he were granting us a generous reprieve. He went back to pacing, his measured steps sounding like the ticking of a clock.

I thought of my in-laws. Did they have any inkling of what was being discussed? What were they feeling as they listened to his boots measuring the floor just above their heads? How did they manage to contain themselves and not rush upstairs to demand a verdict that would put an end to their uncertainty? Or did they still believe that my being a Hutu would save them, that this was just some bureaucratic inconvenience?

He walked over to the shattered picture of my in-laws and pointed. "You know, if they were just a little shorter they could get away as Hutu. You could have bought them fake identity papers."

A lot might have been different were it not for the way those identity cards were designed by the Belgians. There were three designations at the top of each card: *Hutu, Tutsi,* and *Other.* When a card was issued, the word corresponding to the person's origins was circled in dark permanent ink. Once that circle was drawn, a man or woman had nowhere left to hide.

He was in front of my wife now. He bent his head down next to hers and said to her in whispers, "Listen, woman, if you make a big fuss, they will hear downstairs. You will put a terrible fear in them. They will go anyway. There's no question about that, but they will go in fear. If you get up and let my soldiers escort you from the house, it will happen quickly ... a moment of surprise, then a deep rest. Think of it. If you care for them, stay strong, remain quiet, and leave without making a fuss." It was terrifying to listen to his priestly logic.

My wife glanced at me. But there was nothing I could do. My eyes were clouded with sorrow. She turned her eyes away from mine and shut them. When she opened them again a few moments later, she seemed to have gone into a daze and I could no longer feel her as the person I had always known. Like a sleep-walker, she rose from her chair and moved to the front door where she stopped, staring into nothing.

He jumped forward, opened the door for her, and called to the soldiers sitting in the jeep. They ran over, took her by her arms, and led her to the jeep.

I began following her out the door, but he stuck his arm out in front of me like a barricade. He shut the door and pointed to the chair in which I had been sitting. I trudged over and slumped back into the chair. I listened intently, expecting to hear a scream outside.

He walked to the window and parted the curtains. "Your wife is in the jeep. Don't worry, she's safe. She looks comfortable. She has learned to accept. Now it is your turn." What did he mean? What was I to accept? Hadn't I already lost all resistance?

"What do you want?" I asked, careful not to sound as if I were challenging him.

"Acceptance. It's time you accepted that you are a Hutu and not a halfbreed."

"I am a Hutu! And I was even beaten up by Tutsi when I was a young boy," I protested. He smiled and shook his head to discount my words as if I were presenting him a counterfeit identity card! "That was then," he said. "This is now."

He picked up his rifle and began examining it. He checked its chamber and clicked it a few times. "These automatics are amazing machines," he said. "They're faster than a man's mind or body. They no longer run after a man like an ordinary rifle. They speed ahead of him and cut off his run. You can take care of a dozen people with one short burst."

The nausea hit me without warning. I turned my head to one side and threw up my breakfast. He waited for me to recover and then continued as if nothing had happened.

"As I was saying, the important thing for you now is to remember that you are a Hutu and be proud of it." He raised the rifle and held it up sideways, so I could see the length of it, as if he were exhibiting it for inspection at an auction in order to get the bidding started. "There's one trigger and it needs only one finger. The finger presses the trigger and the arm waves the machine from side to side. The machine does the rest. It does its work so well that you can close your eyes while using it."

He shoved the rifle in my arms, totally unconcerned that I might suddenly turn it on him. My arms went numb. Seeing that I was lost with it, he threw his head back and laughed derisively. He took the rifle out of my arms and leaned it against the wall. Then he took the machete off his shoulder strap and held it in front of me.

"This is the finest steel in existence," he said. "In the hands of a real warrior, it can be quicker than an automatic rifle." He laid the machete across my lap.

I could no longer comprehend this torture. Was not my wife already outside the house? Was her mind not numb with defeat and resignation? What else did he want?

"What do you want from me now?" I asked, desperate for some explanation.

And then without the slightest warning, he brought his eyes down on mine with venomous force. His face took on murderous seriousness. "I want you to become a Hutu again! I want you to reclaim your soul and stop shaming your ancestors. First, you sold it to the foreigners, and then to this Tutsi family. I want you to take it back from all of them. I want you to be reborn!"

His voice suddenly took on a fevered urgency. He was breathing hard, insisting, chanting, "You are a Hutu. You will always be a Hutu. Hutu! Kigali! Hutu!"

I thought of them sitting in the basement, waiting, hoping. I saw in my crazed mind their frightened, worried faces. Manna, the mother of my wife, Juvénal, the father of my wife, Sisha, the sister of my wife.

He went on with his litany. "You are a Hutu! Kigali! Hutu! Be a Hutu! You are a Hutu!" His hand was clenched into a fist and it moved up and down to give weight and rhythm to his every word.

And then it was as if his hypnotic gaze flung open some long-locked gate in my mind. I began falling, falling, just like the day they gave me the anaesthetic to operate on my head wounds—the day my friend and I were beaten up by the Tutsi. The surgeon had asked me to count backward from ten—I had slipped into black before reaching the count of four.

I slid deeper into the thick darkness now, falling through it as if it had no beginning or end. From a distance came his hoarse voice, urging me on, "Hutu! You are a Hutu! Hutu! Kigali! Hutu! Be a Hutu!" And then the hissing of the Tutsi boys who had cracked open my skull years ago, "Dirty peasant! You're just a Hutu! You're just a dirty peasant, dirty peasant, dirty peasant."

I felt myself fall through the bottom of the darkness and land on some dusty ground. All around me was a reddish mist and when the mist began to clear I saw that I was on a road. As far as my eyes could see there were long columns of destitute people, trudging in the diseased dust … thousands, hobbling, moving away from their homes. I walked along with the huge throng, my strong legs push-ing me towards the head of the column. Then, suddenly, I recog-nized my wife's family, limping along with all the others. The three of them were stumbling, leaning on one another for strength.

My sister-in-law was the first to see me. She broke out of the column and rushed towards me. She stretched out her hands in supplication. The father and mother peered at me through the cloud of dust and joined their daughter. The three of them fell on their knees before me. Their clothes were torn and ragged, their flesh covered with scabs and flies. My father-in-law pleaded with me to save his wife and daughter. His wife joined in, begged me to leave her there, put some dirt on her head, and save her daughter and husband, instead. The girl wept, begging me to promise not to leave any of them behind.

My nostrils burned from the hot dust, my eyes watered from the merciless glare of the sun. I couldn't stand to hear their sad pleading voices. Why had this burden been placed on me? I was free to roam wherever I wanted without danger, but only because I was not with them. How could they think that this freedom could be shared if I took them under my wing? How was I to make them understand that I too would be branded, like them, the moment I pleaded on their behalf? Did they not see that my own clothes would turn to rags, that my skin would be torn by the same heat, my hopes shattered by the same force that had already shattered theirs? I was an important man only as long as I kept to myself. But I was of no use as a benefactor. My soul and body were no longer mine to do with as I pleased.

But they did not understand. They got up off their knees, stared at me with bitter disappointment, and resumed walking dejectedly with the rest of the column. I walked alongside them, pleading with them to believe me. But they remained mute and stared straight ahead. As the column arrived at a fork in the road, they turned away from the multitude and headed off in the opposite direction. I was unable to tear my eyes off them. I knew that they were doomed to death by disease and destitution if they walked alone, but I felt powerless to stop them, for they continued to ignore me.

They arrived at the top of a sandy hill and began disappearing over it. I scampered to keep up with them. As I crossed over the top of the hill, I stopped, surprised at how the landscape had suddenly changed. The dusty ground had turned into a fertile valley. I glanced down at my feet. They were chalked with dust, and looked pitifully out of place in this fertile grassland. The grass was spiced with the smell of lilies. The sky was a vigorous blue. It was the middle of day and the sun was a burning flame.

I began following the three of them through the green field where there were hundreds of goats grazing, healthy goats that were ready to give milk. As they arrived near a crooked tree around which grazed some of the most handsome goats, my father in law circled the tree and turned around to face me. But I hardly recognized him as he came out from behind the tree. He was tall and walked with princely steps, smooth and measured. He was dressed as a shepherd and held an oil-smooth shepherd's stick.

As I approached him, he lowered his gaze to meet my own and then glanced down at my dusty chapped feet. He looked at me as if I were five hundred years his inferior—he did not feel like kin.

I lowered my eyes and stared at my hands. They were the worn-out hands of a peasant, blistered and crude compared to his sleek smooth hands. I moved closer to him, a bitter rebellion in my heart. But the supreme confidence in his eyes overwhelmed me and I fell to my knees, my dusty feet useless and limp, while he towered over me, in command of the entire countryside.

As the sun glared down at me, I squinted to see him better. Then I saw the two women emerge from behind the tree and turn to face me also. And they too looked different. Both of them were as sleek and confident as he, dressed in fine garments. All three took to gazing at me now with the same pitying looks.

I closed my eyes, hoping that the apparition would disappear into the mist. I prayed that there would be a quick end to this sudden reversal, but they stood their ground and observed my disgrace. It was I who was the unwelcome outsider, I who was the peasant, and they who were lords of the land.

And then I heard a voice from just behind where the three of them were standing. "Be a Hutu! Get on your feet and be a Hutu! Get on your feet like a Hutu! Be a Hutu!"

I strained my eyes against the sun to see who was shouting. It

was my great-grandfather, come from I don't know where, looking as he always had in the portrait in my family's house. He held
a machete above his head, sideways, and I could see the full length
of it, with the sun reflecting off it in short bursts of blinding, mes-
merizing light. His voice was strong and insistent, "This was our
noble weapon before the ferengis arrived with their machines.
This is the only language left now."

He seemed to have emerged from the sun itself, his eyes shining
with fierce proud screams. "Get up on your legs and be a Hutu!
Be a Hutu!" he chanted. And with that, he hurled the machete in
the air and it somersaulted up into the sun, caught its fire, and fell
on the grass in front of where I knelt. I began to protest, but he
disappeared into the glare of the sun.

The man and the two women continued to stand tall, majestic,
unmoved by my dilemma. The green plain was theirs and they
stood on it, owning it and knowing the secrets of its seasons.

And then my legs were pushing up with all their strength. I was
rushing at them and I heard the voice of a wild spirit shouting
from a distance, "Kigali! Kigali! ... Hutu, Kigali! ... Hutu! Kigali!
... Kigali, Imana!" But I knew beyond doubt that it was my own
voice. I knew it from the way the muscles in my throat were
stretching out as far as they could without tearing.

The three of them stood their ground, confident, unperturbed,
proud, just like their ancestors. And only when I threw myself on
them did they look alarmed, surprised and betrayed by my act. I
cut the older woman down first ... and after her the man ... and
after him the younger woman who screamed long terrified wails,
until she fell silent too and there was only the sound of the grazing
goats.

I threw my arms up and chanted, "Kigali! Hutu! ... Hutu!
Kigali." My head felt as if it had become one with the sun. And
out of my golden blindness I saw the blood dripping down the
handle of the machete and onto my raised arms. And then my bewilderment turned to awe as the machete in my hand turned into
a shepherd's stick, well whittled and oil-smooth. I gazed at the fer-

tile land and the healthy goats and I rejoiced that they would be mine forever.

But the fertile grasslands and goats disappeared in a shimmer and I was surrounded again by a reddish mist. The mist began clearing and I found myself standing back in my own living room. The machete slid out of my hand and rattled to the floor. I slumped back into the chair, my vision blurred, my eyes burning with fever. As my eyes began to focus again, I saw him standing exactly where he had been before. He bent down and picked up the machete. He took out a large kerchief from his pocket, wiped the blood off the blade, and tied the machete back to his shoulder strap. He nodded with satisfaction and said, "Now you are reborn. Now, you are a Hutu!"

He went to the door leading to the basement room, shut it, then returned to where I was sitting. He pulled me to my feet, grabbed hold of my bloody shirt, tore it off my back and flung it to the floor. He pushed me to the kitchen sink and poured water over my hands and face. Then he went into the bedroom, brought me a clean white shirt and made me wear it, saying, "There's no need to speak of this to your wife. Tell her it was my doing."

We left the house and began walking to the jeep. I fell in next to my wife and he got in the front passenger seat and motioned for the driver to start up. The third soldier sat next to my wife and me, the barrel of his rifle pointed to the sky. The jeep sped down the street and turned onto the main highway out of Kigali.

We drove without saying a word. My wife leaned her head on my shoulder and remained immobile, staring at but not seeing any of the passing countryside.

Bodies lined both sides of the road. Some were piled in heaps. Others were lined up neatly, wrapped in canvas, ready for the trucks and bulldozers. In some places clouds of black flies swarmed just above the bodies, crashing into one another in their frenzy.

Thousands walked along the road. Streams of misery stretched as far as the eye could see. Most of them were on foot, carrying small bundles. Others pulled old carts piled high with useless things that they had brought with them to remember the homes they would never see again.

Periodically we passed crowded buses that swayed from side to side. There would be as many people hanging on the sides of the bus as there were inside. Occasionally a luxury car would pass through at high speed, gun barrels bristling from the windows.

It was night I think. Or maybe it was day. The jeep came to a stop somewhere. A soldier with fair hair rushed over, lifted my wife out of the jeep, and carried her into a tent. I stumbled after them.

Then I heard his cursed voice right behind me. He was talking to one of the foreign soldiers. I heard him saying something about a woman who was a Tutsi, and how he, a Hutu officer, had delivered her safely. The foreign soldier thanked him for his compassion. I turned to look at him, but he was already in the jeep and it was veering rudely around the other cars, disappearing in the dust in the direction from which we had come.

I fell on a cot. There was a nurse beside me. She put a wet cloth on my forehead. I think I heard her say, "You're safe now. The worst is over."

I woke up a few hours later. My wife was sitting next to me, holding some documents. I took them from her listless hands and read them. They were papers of safe passage. Just then, a French soldier came into the tent and motioned for us to get up. He pointed to a bus parked outside the tent and said, "Burundi. Burundi. Safe. Good refugee camp in Burundi. Away from Rwanda. You go get on the bus now. *Au revoir. Bonne chance.* God be with you."

*

Cyprien stopped speaking. His voice had so filled my mind until then that, at some point, I had closed my eyes in order to see better what he was describing. His abrupt silence brought me back to myself. I opened my eyes and saw him looking at me pleadingly, his head tilted to one side, like the head of a sidewalk beggar hoping to convince one of the innocence of his predicament.

I didn't know what to say. I hesitated for a moment and then said the only thing I could think of saying without belittling his pain. "I'm sorry. I'm really sorry. I'm so goddamned sorry."

"For which one of us?" he asked gently, without irony.

"For every one of you," I answered.

He seemed surprised. "You mean you consider me worthy of sympathy?"

"Maybe there were devils in Kigali. Maybe the dream was not of your own choosing," I said.

"Don't be a fool," he countered. "If Imana is the God of the universe, why did he have no authority over these devils? Why did he let go of his hold over creation? Who chose for all this to happen?"

"Cyprien, that's a question that humankind has always asked itself. I have no answer for it, just as you don't. I asked the same question about Somalia. And I had no answer," I said.

"But there is an answer," he said. "That was no God or devil in me. The dream was an ancient dream, from long before missionaries even began talking of God or the devil. The dream belonged to my ancestors and to a determined soldier standing next to me who had memorized the modern version of it. I heard it told so many times ... the story of the oppressed Hutu, finally rising up defiantly to claim their majority power. My great-great-grandfather dreamed of it and passed it down. The dream was 500 years old, etched in the sun, with its own fire, its own mindless fever. And it turned me into exactly what the soldier wanted me to be: an accomplice with blood on his hands. No God or devil was needed." He added with a weary voice: "I no longer belong to either side. I have fallen outside all sides."

Then I said something very stupid. I don't know why I said it. But it was said and there was nothing I could do about it. I said, "Time will heal. It will be all right."

A wild anger seized him. Beads of perspiration exploded all over his face. He snapped at me, "It's never all right. These things are never all right. It's not a film. It's not a TV serial. You can't change the channel on this one! No! It will never be all right."

He shook his head wistfully, and then threw it back recklessly and broke out into a crazed, raucous laugh. But the laugh lasted for only a moment and collapsed into racking sobs.

I took Cyprien by the hand and led him back to the fountain. I dipped my hands in the water, cupped some of it, and poured it over his face. There was a security guard standing nearby. He walked over and asked me if everything was all right with my friend. I didn't know what to say. I wasn't sure anymore if anything would ever be all right again. Cyprien and I sat on the ledge of the fountain together for some time. I closed my eyes and pondered his story and wondered if it could ever be told, or should be. And then when I opened my eyes a few minutes later he was gone.

Anneh

I had just returned from the fields and was washing my hands. Baba came into the house, cursing. Expecting another one of his harmless tirades, Anneh and my wife retired to the kitchen.

"What's wrong, Baba?" I asked.

"Some people from America," he said. "They've come here looking for relatives. Americans looking for relatives in Turkey! Now the whole village will be talking about it all winter."

I walked out of the house to see the strangers. Umit, my three-year-old boy, wanted to follow me out, but I told my wife to keep him in the house.

I walked down the street and joined a group of villagers who were gathering around a bus. Some foreign women and men were standing in front of the bus listening to a Turkish woman in a blue uniform with a small megaphone in her hand.

She was speaking to them in Turkish. "Please, we must do this in an orderly way. The chief of the village has agreed to allow you to talk to some of the people here, but we must respect the villagers and not overstay our welcome." She then switched to English, probably repeating the same thing she had said a moment earlier. The men and women nodded their heads. Many had tears in their eyes.

The woman in the blue uniform turned to us and said, "These ladies and gentlemen are from the United States. They have come to Turkey looking for relatives lost many years ago. They will be staying for the afternoon. We ask that you be good hosts. They have come a long way. Most of them do not speak Turkish, but I am here to interpret."

The group began walking down the street, stopping to talk Armenian to some of the men and women who stood outside their homes. The men and women stared back at them warily, not understanding. I knew they were talking in Armenian because some Armenians had settled near our village; many times I had heard them talking together when they came to buy things from the stores.

I fell in and walked with them, trying to make sense of their visit. At one house, one of the women in the group approached a man about my own age, showed him a photograph, and asked him something. The father of the man stepped in and, gesticulating violently, scolded the woman. She told him through the interpreter that she was looking for her boy, that it was a mother's right to keep looking until she found her only son. The father replied angrily to the interpreter that the woman had better move on down the street. The interpreter took the woman gently by the arm and moved her along to the next house.

One of the women from the bus fell into step beside me. She was in her early thirties and was wearing a pretty dress. I was taken by surprise when she turned to me speaking in fluent Turkish. She said that this was a difficult experience for her, ours being the fifth village she had visited that week.

"Are you Turkish?" I asked.

"I'm Armenian. I've lived in America for many years. But I was born here in Turkey. The Armenian family that adopted me in America spoke Turkish very well. I asked my adopted father to speak it to me. I knew I would come back one day."

"Were you born in this region?" I asked.

"Yes, not very far away. But they found us two hundred kilometres to the north of here, on the road to Syria."

"Found you? When?" I asked, not understanding her meaning.

"Fifteen years ago. Most died during the long march. They told us they were relocating us, that our lands would be rented and the money credited to accounts opened in our names. They promised they would bring us back to our villages after the war. First they took the men away, and then a few weeks later they took the rest of us from our village. We walked for days, without any food. They drove us like cattle, without pity, waiting for us to die from exhaustion. Some Turkish families tried to give us food on the way, but the soldiers shot anyone who tried to help us. Only a few of us were left when the British found us."

"Whose soldiers? Why?" I asked in bewilderment.

She looked at me as if I were asking a foolish question, a question to which I should already have the answer.

"I had a brother," she continued. "But they took him away from me minutes before we set out on the long march."

"I'm sorry," I said.

"All I have left of my childhood is a family portrait of my mother, my brother and me. I hid it under my shawl when they took us from our village. We weren't allowed to take anything with us, but I took our picture."

"What happened to your mother?" I asked, not certain whether it was the respectful thing to ask.

She began weeping uncontrollably. She took a handkerchief out of her bag and wiped her reddened eyes. "My poor brother was with my mother when ... " She broke into tears again and pulled herself together with great effort. "My brother was too young and couldn't understand. Poor Andranik sat next to her, talking to her ... "

There had been some talk in our village about a war with the Armenians but no one spoke much about it, and our history lessons didn't mention it.

"I'm very sorry," I said, lowering my head. "I didn't know about any of this. They never told us about it in school."

She reached in her bag and pulled out a picture. "This was my mother," she said. She hesitated, made the sign of the Christian cross over her forehead, and handed me the picture.

I took it from her out of politeness. It was an oval picture yellowed with age of a young beautiful woman with her two children.

I stared at the picture and was drawn into the young woman's kind eyes. I slowed, came to a stop and leaned against a tree. I continued to look into the young woman's eyes, unable to tear myself away from them.

I heard the trembling voice of the woman who had given me the picture asking, "What is it? What do you see?"

"Nothing," I replied, coming back to myself. I handed her back the picture. "Your mother had very kind eyes."

"*Ke hooshyes?*" she suddenly asked in Armenian, searching my face for a reaction.

"I'm sorry," I answered. "I do not understand."

She switched back to Turkish. "Do you remember? Andranik? Are you Andranik?"

"No, I am Seljuk," I answered, wishing I had stayed in the house.

She looked at me suspiciously. "Are you sure?"

"Of course, I'm sure. My name is Seljuk. I've lived here all my life. I'm Muslim."

She wasn't convinced. "No, you are Andranik! I know you are Andranik. I can feel it!" Sweat was pouring down her trembling face.

I raised my voice in defiance. "No, I told you. I'm a Muslim!"

She shook her head and began telling me about her village and how she and I used to go to a waterfall and how I fell into the pool, how one of my cousins saved me and then broke his leg while carrying me back to the house. She told me how our mother used to take me by the hand every morning and walk me to the chicken coop so I could pick out a fresh egg for my breakfast. She told me about the tall mountains that surrounded the village.

"Leave me alone!" I shouted. "Have you gone mad? I don't remember any of this. I am Muslim. I told you. I am Muslim! I can't be the person you want me to be. Leave me alone!"

She stopped and looked around, as if searching for some new way to say what she had already said. Then suddenly she took me by the hand and pulled me down with her to the sandy ground. She held my index finger and began to write in the sand. Faintly a distant voice was calling "*Akhper! Akhper!*"

"What is this writing?" I asked.

She answered, "*Akhper, Akhper*," and pulling the picture hurriedly from her bag, she thrust it into my hands.

I looked at the woman in the picture and couldn't tear my eyes from hers. My heart pounded wildly, as I struggled to my feet gasping for air. I leaned against the tree, but my legs wouldn't support me and I slid down the rough bark, still holding onto the picture. The small boy in the picture seemed to be looking into the secret part of me, knowing my every thought.

I felt something terrifying was about to happen that I was helpless to escape. Alternately hot and cold, my body drenched in sweat, I felt my village disappearing from around me. Some eye deep within me stared into a different time and place. Suddenly the air was the crisp cold of autumn, and the sounds and smells of a village I did not know came to me with a terrible familiarity. I was walking with my mother on the road leading out of our village. The soldiers had taken all the women and children from our houses, gathered us in the village square and then ordered us to march out of the village. She was carrying me, crying, holding me tightly to her bosom. "Don't be afraid, my rose petal, everything will be all right," she whispered in my ear. Next to us were my aunt and my older sister.

One of the soldiers walking alongside us came up to my mother and said to her in a gruff voice, "Put him down. He's old enough. Let him walk on his own. If you carry him you'll be exhausted soon. We can't be slowing down just for you. Put him down!"

My mother held on to me even tighter and answered, "He is my son. You took my husband away from me. I will not let you take my son, too."

The soldier grabbed her by the sleeve of her overcoat and dragged us away from the group. He slapped my mother on her face. "I said put him down!"

She put me down and wrapped her overcoat around me to protect me from the soldier. I clung to her dress. The soldier then pulled my mother and me off the road and into the field. I hung onto her skirts, burying my face in her belly. She was breathing hard. I could feel her heart beating wildly. She was shouting at him, "You took my husband. Our village. What else do you want? What did we ever do to you?"

Then I heard the sound of metal being unsheathed and a frightening swishing sound cut through the air. My mother stood still for a moment, then slowly sank to the ground with me still holding onto her skirts. I cried, "Mairik, what is wrong, Mairik? Stand up, Mairik." The soldier towered over us, long sword in hand, eyes red with fury.

I got up and grabbed her arm and tried to pull her back to her feet. Tugging on her arm, I noticed that she was also lying a few feet away. I looked down at her and then over at her. I couldn't understand. I walked over the few feet to her and knelt in the mud and looked into her eyes. I touched her lips and said repeatedly, *"Mairik, inchoo chyes khosoom?"* repeating over and over again, "Mama, why aren't you speaking?" She remained silent and continued looking at me, her eyes filled with concern.

I brushed my fingers against the soft skin of her face. I whispered, "Mairik, get up. Let us hurry back to the others. They are calling us. We have to go back." I took a lock of her long brown hair and gave it a gentle pull. Her head turned slightly and her eyes locked with mine, but she did not get up.

Another soldier arrived at our side. "You have to join the others now," he said to me in Turkish. "Get up," he insisted. "Everyone is going to march down the road. You have to go with them. Get up or you'll be left behind, there will be wolves here at night."

"Is my mother coming?" I asked. "She can't stay here with the wolves."

"No. She's going to stay here for now. She will come later," he said, lifting me and shoving me back towards the road.

I stumbled back to the spot where my mother was lying on the wet earth, her overcoat covered with mud. I stopped and looked at her. Her legs were my mother's legs, her back was my mother's back and the shawl covering her shoulders was my mother's shawl. I turned and trudged back to where I had sat and looked into her eyes. I knelt down in the mud and looked into her eyes again and said, "Wake up, Mairik. We have to go back. Why aren't you getting up? We have to go back to the others. Please get up and come." I touched her lips, but still she did not speak. "Why aren't you getting up, Mairik?" I cried, louder now, hoping my voice would wake her.

I then lifted her carefully and walked with her to where she was lying in the mud. I knelt down and put her head back with the rest of her, drawing the collar of her overcoat around her neck to keep her warm.

"Mairik? They are waiting! The man is angry! Hurry and wake up, Mairik!" I said, my seven-year-old heart beating wildly.

Some of the people called out to me, urging me to hurry and return to the group. "Andranik, Andranik, come, Andranik!" they shouted.

The soldier lifted me, draped me over his shoulder, and carried me back to the group. My sister tried to take me in her arms, but I pulled back. She sobbed in Armenian, *"Akhper. Meir Mairike genats. Meir Mairike genats. Akhper Andranik! Inch ke anienk hima?"* Several times she repeated, "Brother Andranik! Our mother is gone. What shall we do now?"

"I tried to wake her, but she is still asleep," I answered.

She turned to an older woman next to her and said, "My poor brother has lost his mind." Puzzled, I looked at the older woman's face. She was also weeping. She put her arms around me, lifted me up, and held me tightly to her bosom. I turned my head and shouted across the field, "Mairik, get up and come. There are wolves at night."

We were still walking the next day. My feet were caked with mud. The older woman would carry me for awhile and then set me down. I would walk for a distance till my legs couldn't bear it any more. Then she would pick me up again and carry me until my weight became too much for her own bleeding feet. Once in awhile, someone would collapse on the road and the soldiers would order the rest of us to keep on marching.

We reached a fork in the road and the men with the rifles and swords ordered us to come to a stop. One of them talked in Turkish, while another translated his words into Armenian, "You will divide here. Those who are over eight years old will take the road to the right. Those eight or under will take the road to the left." Then he said to the adults, "The children will be taken care of. You will be reunited with them later. They will be brought to you when you arrive at your new homes. They are too young to walk with you. They will only slow you down."

Hearing these words many of the women took to weeping and shouting and hurried to hide their children behind their skirts. But the soldiers ignored their pleas and passed through the group, collecting us children and making us stand in a single file away from the others. My sister began waving at me desperately, calling out, "*Akhper! Akhper!*" Someone pulled her back, and she disappeared into the group, still screaming.

The older people were led down the road that turned to the right. Occasionally, some of the women would turn around and try to run back to us, but the soldiers would hit them with their rifles and force them to keep walking. After awhile, the last of them disappeared around the bend in the road. And a short while later, I couldn't hear their weeping or shouts anymore.

We stood on the road in single file, some of the youngest shivering and crying. A truck arrived and two soldiers lifted us and put us in. One of the soldiers climbed in and sat on the bench in front of me. He smiled at me and made a funny face, twirling his long mustache with his fingers. Even though I was trembling, I smiled back.

The soldier said to me in Turkish, "Don't be afraid. Don't worry. Best to forget. We're taking you to a good place, a nice village far from here where there's a running river and many children to play with."

"Where did the others go?" I asked, pointing back to the road.

"The others are going far from here. They have a long way to walk. They're going where they will work," he replied. I stared back, not understanding. He repeated it a second time.

"Why would they go work somewhere else without taking the donkeys and sheep with them?" I asked.

He didn't answer.

"Why aren't they taking any food with them?" I asked.

Again he didn't answer.

"Is there food where they are going?" I asked.

"Yes, lots of food. Big gardens, full of fruit."

"How far will they have to walk to get there?"

"A week, maybe three, if some fall sick."

"Why would some fall sick?"

"It's a long way. Some will fall sick."

"Will the rest take care of them?"

He turned his head and glanced at the other children in the truck. Then he turned back to me and said, "Don't ask so many questions. It's not good to ask so many questions."

He didn't speak to me anymore until we reached a village. When the truck came to a stop, he lifted me off and walked me to a house. Some other soldiers took the other children further down the street to other houses. I could hear the children asking questions in Armenian.

The house to which the soldier took me had a green door. He knocked impatiently. A woman opened the door. She looked at us questioningly.

Speaking in Turkish, he ordered her to let us in.

The woman answered, "No, he can't come in. He's an Armenian. I don't want trouble. Find another house. Take him somewhere else."

The soldier raised his voice. "Let us in, I said!"

The woman lowered her head and didn't move. The soldier pushed her aside and walked into the house, pulling me by my hand.

"Where's your husband?" he asked the woman.

"He's in the fields. He'll be home soon, and he won't like this," she said, not looking him in the face.

"He doesn't have to like it. He has nothing to say about it. We are the government now. We are the ones who decide," answered the soldier. He sat down on a chair and pointed out another chair for me to sit on. I sat on the edge of the chair. My legs couldn't reach the floor. I reached forward to touch the floor with my feet but slipped off the chair. I climbed back and sat still.

"All you and your husband need do is treat him like you would any Turkish child. Feed him and clothe him. Take him to the fields with you, and to the mosque every Friday. His life begins here, today. He's only seven, young enough to forget. He will forget soon. But he asks a lot of questions. Don't answer any of them unless they have to do with this village. Treat him as if he had always lived here. He will forget soon."

He then asked the woman to bring him some tea. She went over to a samovar, poured some tea in a glass, dropped in two sugar cubes, and handed it to him. He told her to fetch me something too. She disappeared into another room and reappeared with a glass of milk. She handed me the glass of milk and said in Turkish, "Don't spill any of it and don't slurp while you drink." I drank the milk, keeping my lips clamped tight around the edge of the glass so no one would hear me swallowing. It was the first food I had tasted since leaving my village.

A man walked in the front door. He stopped and stared wide-eyed at me. Then he turned to the soldier and said, "What are you doing here? Who is this boy? Is he one of the Armenian children you brought here tonight? The whole village is talking about it. Have you gone crazy?"

The soldier stood up. "You will raise him as a Turk. He is young. He will forget soon."

The man answered, "I already pay a share of my crop to your troops. What else should I owe you? Leave me out of it. We have no quarrel with you or them. Take your share of the crop, but leave us out of it."

The soldier shook his head. "Crops alone won't make for a greater Turkish nation. You must keep the boy and raise him as a Turk."

"And what's in it for us?" asked the man.

"Your country's honour, the pride of a greater Turkey. Isn't that enough? But since you're a peasant and don't think beyond your own village, you'll be given a sack of potatoes every month. It will help pay for his keep."

"Does the little fellow speak Turkish?" asked the man, glancing briefly in my direction. I looked down at my dangling legs.

"He understands. He may not speak it well, but he knows enough to be asking questions he shouldn't be asking. Don't answer any questions that have anything to do with his past."

"What happened in his village?" asked the man. "What did you do to them?" The soldier motioned for him to be silent.

The woman went into another room and returned a few minutes later with some pastries. She gave me one and then wrapped a few for the soldier to take away with him. I held my pastry in the palm of my hand. I wanted to eat it, but I was afraid I'd drop the crumbs. The soldier thanked the woman, got up, and walked over to me. He ruffled my hair with his hand and said, "Don't ask too many questions. Look and learn from the other children." He said goodnight to the man and woman and left the house.

When the soldier had gone, the woman told me that I was going to live there with her and that I was to call her Anneh. Over the next few days I heard the boys and girls in the village calling their mothers Anneh and I began doing the same.

That first night, Anneh led me up a small staircase in the back of the house to a small room in the attic. She told me I had to be very careful going up and down the stairs, not to fall down.

She unrolled a mattress on the floor, opened a chest, took out some sheets, spread them over the mattress, and covered the sheets with a blanket. She told me to get under the covers. Then she walked over to a small window and opened its curtain to let in the moonlight. She stared at me for a few moments and walked back downstairs.

I waited for awhile and got out from under the covers. I crawled to the top of the stairs. I heard her and the man talking. The man was shouting, saying that he wanted nothing to do with the war. She was saying that everybody had got along fine before the army stuck its nose in it. The man continued complaining until she told him to be quiet. "Keep your voice down or he will hear and will not forget." Soon the lights went off and there was silence.

I crawled back to the mattress and pulled the sheets over my head. I drifted off to sleep whispering Armenian words, softly, so no one would hear me: *bariev* hello, *kar* stone, *hatz* bread, *gelkhark* hat, *toon* home, *katoo* cat, *havgit* egg, *khaghalik* toy.

The next morning Anneh gave me new clothes to wear and told me to go and play in the garden. I left the house and sat on a wooden bench just outside the front door. Some older boys walked up to the house. They surrounded me. One of them reached out and touched my hair, but withdrew his hand quickly and wiped it on his shirt. The other boys looked at each other and burst out laughing.

Anneh came out of the house, cursed them and told them that they would all go to hell. They ran off laughing. She lifted me up and took me back into the house. She sat me at the table, gave me a biscuit and a glass of milk. Watching me eat the biscuit, she said, "You will forget soon. Tell me. What is your name?"

"Andranik," I answered.

"Your name is Seljuk," she said. "And I am your Anneh."

She had me repeat my name a few times. Then she began weeping softly, reached over and caressed my hair. I could not understand why she was weeping but the biscuit was good and I felt hungry.

A couple of days later, some of the children who had been brought to the village with me walked over to the house and spoke to me in Armenian. But Anneh heard us and scolded us for talking in Armenian. She sent the other children away and took me back in the house. This happened several more times over the next few days. And then we understood that if we talked Armenian to each other, we would be taken back into our houses and wouldn't be allowed to play outside. So we didn't talk to each other in Armenian anymore. We looked at each other without speaking and played silently. But we didn't like to stay quiet, so after awhile we began talking to each other in Turkish.

In the beginning, every night before falling asleep, I repeated Armenian words in my mind. But late one night, Anneh came up to my room to bring some clean sheets. She noticed I was awake and asked me why I wasn't asleep yet. After that, I was afraid that she might hear my mind. So I stopped repeating the Armenian words.

After a few weeks, the older boys in the village stopped making fun of me. They took me fishing and taught me things. I went to school and learned to read and write Turkish. I helped Baba in the fields and, on Friday mornings, I went to the mosque with him.

*

Some villagers had gathered around me. One of them was throwing cold water on my face. I could hear my sister's voice crying, "*Akhper, Akhper!*" One of the villagers was saying to another, "Poor Seljuk has lost his head. He's been rolling on the ground, babbling in Armenian." He bent down and tried to take the picture out of my hand, but I clutched it fiercely.

Struggling to my feet, I leaned against the tree wiping my face with my sleeve, desperately trying to focus through the haze of nausea that churned through my body. As I stepped away from the tree, legs trembling, the villagers who had gathered around me moved back to make way for me. I saw the green door of our house in the distance. My wife, my son and Anneh were hurrying down the road. Baba was following them leaning on his cane.

I began stumbling in their direction, then came to a stop, no longer certain of which way to go. An instant later, I felt my son's arms hugging my shaky legs. Then Anneh was standing in front of me, face pale, eyes filled with worry. Behind me, I could hear my sister crying, "*Akhper, Akhper.*" Once again, I looked at the photo and into Mairik's eyes, hoping her voice would send me a message, but there was only silence.

Dasvidania

It was a perfect October late afternoon in Moscow. The tree-tops glowed orange in the setting sun. I paused a moment to watch them coming towards me. He was a good looking young man walking beside a young woman who was pushing one of those baby carriages with the pull-down tops, like the ones from the 50's. She took small quick steps on her high heels leaning over the carriage, trying to talk to the baby without tripping.

Just as they passed me, she turned to her companion and said in Russian, "We have to feed him first. It wouldn't be right if we didn't feed him first. I can't if we don't feed him first."

I turned and looked at them, wondering what she meant. Lingering, I pulled a map of Moscow out of my pocket and did my best to look lost.

They stopped in front of a restaurant. She stayed with the carriage while he hurried inside. Wondering what he could find in a restaurant to feed an infant, I walked over to the restaurant and went in.

He was saying something to the waiter. The waiter nodded and went to a fridge placed at the far end of the counter. I asked the cashier for a Snickers™ candy bar. The young man sat on a bar stool and fiddled with a set of keys to which was attached a minia-ture Ninja Green-Turtle™ vinyl flashlight. He turned the turtle-light on and off repeatedly, jabbing his thumb on its soft rubbery back. His eyes scanned the walls decorated with autographed pic-tures of sports celebrities. A couple of the celebrities were smiling proudly, holding newborn babies in their arms.

The waiter returned to the counter carrying a can of Coke™ and two straws. The young man paid the waiter, left the straws on the counter and walked out with the can of Coke™. I waited a few moments and followed him out.

They were standing by the carriage arguing. He had a baby bottle in his hand and was filling it with the Coke™.

"Why didn't you get him milk?" she asked.

"He's just thirsty. Coke will do fine," he replied.

He poured the rest of the Coke™ into the bottle and screwed back its Playtex™ nipple. He turned the bottle upside down and squeezed the nipple—a jet of liquid spurted out. He stuck the nipple in the baby's mouth. A pair of tiny hands reddened by the cold of autumn grasped the bottle gently.

"You're crazy. Why didn't you ask for milk? What was so damned complicated, so impossible about getting milk?"

"It doesn't make a difference. I've never been in a restaurant to order milk. If you wanted milk, you could have gone in yourself."

"You could have said the milk was for your baby," she argued.

He leaned to within an inch of her face, arched his eyebrows, and spoke deliberately and slowly, "Maybe I didn't want the waiter to know that I let myself be tricked into having a baby."

She threw her head back defiantly, as if to shake his words out of her mind. He pointed to the baby in the carriage. "There. See? He's drinking it just fine. I told you he would drink it. He'll be drinking vodka in no time." He started to laugh, but cut the laugh short and smiled at her a little sheepishly. She stayed silent, lips turned down in contempt. He said to her in an endearing voice, "We'll be all right. Don't worry. We'll be all right."

She shook her head in mock despair, like a mother on the verge of forgiving her repentant boy. "Do you think he's all right? Do you think he's going to be all right? I'm not joking now. Will he be all right?"

"Of course he'll be all right. He'll always be all right. No need to worry like that."

He put his right arm round her shoulder and she draped her left arm around his waist and let it slide down just below his belt. He looked over to where I was standing. He grinned at me and nodded. "Amerikanski?" he asked, pointing to the map in my hand.

"No, I'm Canadian," I answered.

"Canada. Da! Canada very good country. Number one country! You are tourist?" he said.

"Yes and no. I'm a writer."

"You read writer Solzhenitsyn?" he asked.

"Yes, he is a great writer."

"He is also good witness," he added, with grave respect. "You are witness writer too? You write witness about Russia today? Is not good here. Is terrible. But better than Stalin's Russia. But still terrible."

"You have a nice baby," I said.

"Our baby," he answered, hesitantly, glancing at the young woman.

"Nice talking with you. Dasvidania."

"Da, Dasvidania." The woman smiled faintly, nodding her head just a little.

I was about to walk on when a limousine pulled up in front of them. For a moment I wondered if they weren't celebrities out for a quiet walk—maybe they had an appointment here with their chauffeur. I had seen youngsters strutting around Moscow with tens of thousands of dollars in their pockets. It wouldn't have surprised me.

They turned to face the limousine. The driver jumped out looking around furtively. He opened the back door and a man and woman in their mid-forties stepped out. Both were dressed elegantly. The man stuck his hands in the pockets of his overcoat and nodded impatiently to the driver. The driver glanced suspiciously at me. I looked down at the map in my hands and crossed to the other side of the road.

The driver reached into the car and pulled out a briefcase, then walked over and handed the case to the young man. The young man took the case and propped it on the hood of the baby carriage. He snapped it open, looked at its contents for a few seconds, then snapped it shut. He leaned over the carriage tucking the case behind the pillow, then picked up the baby. He stepped forward, handed the baby to the driver, then stepped back and stood next to the young woman. She leaned against him, weeping softly.

The driver walked back to the couple standing next to the limousine and passed the baby to the woman. She cradled the baby, rocked him, said a sweet word to him, and then passed him to the man standing next to her. He took the baby in his arms, smiled, nodded his head in approval, and passed the baby back to the woman. The woman clutched the baby to her and took a few hesitant steps towards the young woman, stopped, opened her mouth to say something, and then suddenly turned and walked back to the limousine. All three climbed in and as the motor started a window was lowered. The woman stuck her arm and head out, waved, and said in an American accent, "Good luck. Dasvidania." The tinted window rolled back up. The car lurched forward and sailed down the street.

The young couple stood very still watching the car disappear around the corner. Then the young man turned to the baby carriage and lifted out the briefcase. He opened it and looked at its contents again before snapping it shut. He tucked the briefcase under his left arm and began walking. He stopped and looked back at the young woman. The young woman hesitated for a second. Then she put her hand on the handle of the empty carriage and began pushing it down the road. They walked forlornly one next to the other, neither saying a word.

When they reached the end of the street, the young woman gave the carriage a sharp push. As it hit the edge of the pavement it toppled over, spilling baby blankets into the muddy street. The young man put his arm around the young woman. Her body arched toward his as they turned the corner.

Ten and a Half Ounces Per Day

December 18, 1972—The first few callers ask for him by name, hoping to shout their curses directly in his own ear. But his wife handles the phone and becomes adept at managing them. Then the calls arrive in perfect formation, men and women, one on the heels of the other, as if they are taking turns using the same telephone.

"Hello, tell that husband of yours he doesn't know what he's talking about. Tell him to put his greedy ambitions aside," says one.

"Do you buy groceries for your family? Be careful shopping for food these days. Some of the food is contaminated," warns another with an unholy cackle.

"I was in the camps. I was a guard. Why is he ruining our reputations like this? We served the nation. We were patriots."

"I read his works. I used to admire him. But he is worse than scum now."

"His books should be burned and he along with them."

His wife finds a way to unnerve the callers. She throws them off balance with biting sarcasm. She asks one of them how much he is paid to make such phone calls. With another, she waits till he has finished delivering his vitriol and then asks him politely to give the head of the KGB a message from her and her husband.

Their children are still toddlers and have no inkling of what this is all about. Hearing the phone ringing incessantly, they think this a normal part of being in the world.

Next day, comes a warning from the *New York Times*: "This campaign may now do the USSR more harm than the publication of

137

the book itself." But the State continues spreading its malice, convinced it is the best and only reaction. A few blocks away from his Moscow apartment, giant effigy posters are hung near Gorky street, denouncing and ridiculing him and his work.

And then the offensive ceases just as suddenly as it had begun. The phone calls stop altogether. There are no more attacks in the press. There is an eerie silence.

He thinks—I've always been prepared for the worst, always expected them to arrest me without warning. But maybe they've come to their senses and realized they can't arrest me without triggering worldwide indignation.

He and his wife put the children to bed and begin rehearsing where exactly each of them will stand should the police suddenly rush into their apartment.

"You stand to the left, where you can keep an eye on them in case any of them head for the bedroom. I'll stand next to the work desk and make sure they don't slip a bogus piece of evidence under some of the papers," he says to his wife.

February 11, 1973—There's a knock on the door. He leaves the safety latch on and opens the door. The caller sticks his foot in the opening, saying that he has a document for him. He opens the door and a young man steps in, clumsy and nervous, anxious to collect a signature and return to the safety of his superiors. He presents a summons and asks him to sign it and show up at the Prosecutor's Office.

He takes the paper from the young man, walks over to his desk, writes a short response to the summons, and sticks the response across the space reserved for his signature. Then, firmly and politely, with the calmness of an unworried man, he tells the young messenger that he won't sign the paper nor come of his own free will. The bewildered young man snatches the summons and stumbles out of the apartment.

After all, they have sent only one man. As far as he's concerned, one messenger delivering a summons isn't enough to constitute force. If he were voluntarily to sign the summons and agree to report he would be acknowledging the legitimacy of their authority and submitting to it. He thinks—if they are really determined, they will come after me with more men. Only when they come to take me by force will I relent and go with them. Only then will it be clear for all the world to see that their only power over a free person is the power of brute muscle.

He walks into the bedroom and puts together a prison kit. He remembers the dismal facilities in prison years ago, how precious were a couple of bars of soap where a prisoner had no rights—except to ten and a half ounces of bread per day.

February 12, 1973—A series of insistent knocks on the door. He opens it as far as the latch will allow. A foot quickly jams the opening. A strict voice says that there's a matter to be cleared up about the summons. It won't take long, just a formality.

He opens the door. Two men fling it open the rest of the way and walk in boldly. They push him down the small hallway that leads back to the living room, falling in, shoulder to shoulder, blocking his view of the door. Six other men pour into the apartment. He motions to his wife and they quickly get into position to keep their eyes on all eight men.

The men seem to have no intention of searching the apartment. The leader of the group, dressed impeccably, has a dossier in his hand which he opens stiffly, looking like a monarch about to read from a throne speech. He announces that he is a senior Counsellor. "You are to come with me. Sign here," he demands, holding out the dossier and a pen.

"I will not sign," he replies, handing the officer back the dossier and the pen. But he knows that, although he can continue to refuse to sign his own name to his persecution, he can no longer refuse to be taken in for interrogation. They have at last come to take him by force. He can submit to this without betraying his conscience.

"I will not sign. But I will come," he says.

The officer looks surprised for an instant, as if he had heard something totally out of character. The prisoner turns and heads for the bedroom. The officer hurries after him, perhaps worried that his ward might jump headlong out the window. When he sees him gathering his prison kit, he snaps, "There's no need to exaggerate the whole thing. You'll be back here in two hours."

He puts on an old sheepskin coat, carefully hanging his better coat back in his closet. "Why are you putting on that old coat when you have a good fur coat?" demands the officer.

"These are my prison clothes," he answers, knowing it will irritate the man that much more. He walks back into the living room, with the officer following a close step behind. The men all keep their eyes on him. His work table is covered with papers and manuscripts, yet no one in the group seems much concerned with them.

The eight men gather around him now crowding him towards the door. He reaches over the human barricade and makes the sign of the cross over his wife's forehead. She does the same for him. Some of the men flinch, as if they find this simple gesture far more disturbing than all the pages of his books put together.

The door of the KGB car is already open. They push him in and sit on either side of him. On the journey he looks out the window and surveys the street signs to figure out where they're headed. Then a familiar turn and he recognizes the Lefortovo prison.

They bundle him up the stairs and through a cheerless hall with cold dead walls, as if someone has carefully gone through the place and ensured that every inch of it was painted the precise tint of hopelessness.

New little body-search rooms now, different from the ones at Lubyanka years ago. A body searcher arrives, cheerful and efficient, not at all brutal, a competent specialist. His clothes are removed and he's given a prison tunic, shoes without laces, and, of all things, a suit. He would prefer to keep his sweater and coat. But he's told that his clothes have to be sent for disinfecting.

Then the familiar walk down the hallway and into a cell. Not a solitary cell as he would have expected. His cellmate is a young man, imprisoned on charges of small currency trafficking. The young man asks him for his name. He tells him. But the young man has never heard of him.

Again, the infernal ceiling light. Day and night, always on, just as it was years ago. Once more, the shoes without laces so a prisoner won't hang himself and put an end to his misery, and the cheap blanket that sheds on contact, covering anything it touches with a riot of lint.

The food wagon has come and gone already, and some black bread remains on the table. The young man offers him some. He takes a small piece and begins chewing on it. It's better than the bread he was fed in Lubyanka years ago, but it still tastes like soggy clay.

Nine o'clock. Four hours have passed since they took him from his apartment, assuring his wife they'd have him back in two. A jangle of keys again. A lieutenant-colonel motions him to follow.

Down the hall. Dim ceiling lights covered in metal casings everywhere, then a door, turn right, go in. A stronger light now. A voice orders him to sit in the chair that's been placed in front of the interrogation desk. Some men are sitting in a row at the back of the room, as if put there to prevent him from getting up and running back through some time warp.

"Solzhenitsyn?" asks the man standing behind the desk.

"The same," he answers.

"Alexsandr Isayevich?" as if to make sure it is no other.

"Quite so."

The interrogator introduces himself, sounding like a prince who has arrived incognito in a village square and suddenly decided to impress everyone by revealing his true identity: "Malyarov. Deputy Prosecutor General of the U.S.S.R."

Malyarov reads him the charge, citing Article 64.

"What's that?" asks the prisoner, pretending not to know the law.

"Treason," answers the prosecutor, doing his best to conceal his irritation. He shows him the paper, "Sign here."

For a long time he has prepared for this, decided exactly what words to use. "I shall take no part in this. I shall take no part in your investigation or in your trial. Go ahead and carry on without me," he says firmly.

The prosecutor doesn't look surprised. "Sign the paper then, just to show you have been informed," he says.

"I have said everything I am going to say," replies the prisoner.

The prosecutor signs the paper himself to show that the proceedings have begun. Without asking him any further questions, they take him back to his cell. A normal procedure, he tells himself; the real interrogation could last two or more months.

Lying on the cot in the cell he remembers March 9, 1953.

*

Recently released from prison, he suffered from insomnia contracted in the work camps. He had fallen asleep only minutes before dawn, lying with his blanket tucked under his feet, a habit from his days in the icy prison camp barracks where prisoners slept with their feet stuck in the sleeves of their jackets to keep their blood from thickening.

The old woman who lived next door to him ran into his room and shook him awake. "Wake up. Open your eyes. Something has happened. Come outside quickly. Hurry now," she shouted.

She pulled him out of bed, then waited in the hallway for him to get dressed. Grabbing him by the sleeve she pulled him out into the street where a crowd had gathered around a military truck. A grey loudspeaker mounted on the truck blared out the news.

"The Leader is dead. The Comrade in Arms is gone. The Leader and Teacher of the Workers of the World, Coryphaeus of the Sciences, the Mountain Eagle, the Best Friend of the Children, has died."

He held his breath while listening to the official obituary. Then he breathed again, not altogether recognizing this new breath.

The old woman tugged at his sleeve impatiently. He bent his head close to hers and said in a voice just loud enough to reach her deaf ear as a whisper: "It's Stalin. Stalin has died. Stalin is dead."

The old woman nodded, then smiled—the stoic smile of a person who had just heard that the man who sent her son a thousand miles away to his death was dead.

A military dirge bellowed over the loudspeaker now. The crowd stood immobile for a little while longer. Then the driver of the truck started the engine and headed off, leaving the people in a trail of dust.

He didn't return directly to his room. He joined the crowd headed for the village tea shop. Entering the tea shop, he picked a table off to one side, and listened to the grim looking men who were talking in hushed voices. If any of them were overjoyed, they had managed to clamp a convincing mask of grief over their faces.

Some of the men were badly shaken. "What will we do now?" they asked, searching one another's faces for reassurance.

The same question was being repeated in hundreds of cities, towns and villages: "What will we do now?" In Moscow, they were preparing to project a giant picture of Stalin into the night sky. Within a few hours, the crowds, hearing the military marches broadcast over the rooftops, would pour into the streets. They would look up at the floodlit heavens, see Stalin's face, and become hysterical.

He slipped a cube of sugar into his mouth and swallowed some of the hot tea. He wondered if Stalin's death would make much difference. After all, the prisons would remain where they were. The condemned would continue to serve the remainder of their sentences—some had as much as twenty years left. The same guards would tower over the people as they had always done. They would still wear the comfortable felt boots made by the prisoners and would continue to exact a price for favours, such as a few hours of sick leave. A prisoner would continue having no saviour except his own wits.

He took another sip of the tea and remembered the foul yellowish liquid that used to pass for food in the camps. He remembered how men, driven to desperation, licked the food residue off each other's plates, how a prisoner went around mooching morsels from those fortunate enough to receive food parcels from their families.

Yes, it's as if the man of steel had held on, even past his allotted time, just to make sure his apparatus was firmly in place.

Walking back to his rented room he felt as if this were his first day of freedom as a man, although not as a writer. At the school where he taught mathematics and physics, he maintained a scrupulous silence about his literary work. His students considered him brilliant and dedicated, able to present the most complicated mathematical concepts in comprehensible ways. But none of them knew that he wrote when he was alone. Even though he was well liked, he kept to himself, arrived a minute or two before the start of a class and left promptly when he finished teaching. He never showed any interest in topics outside of mathematics and physics. Whenever the conversation drifted to literature, he pretended to be indifferent to it.

Returning to his room at the end of each day, he bolted the door, drew the curtains. He walked over to his dresser, opened a drawer, and retrieved some papers hidden under his clothing. He sat at his table, sharpened his pencils, and continued writing where he had left off the day before.

He used the thinnest paper he could find. He had developed a miniature handwriting to squeeze as much text in as few pages as possible. He kept no margins, filling the pages, leaving little space between the lines. He didn't measure his manuscripts in terms of number of words or pages, but in terms of the cubic space needed to conceal them. He hid what he wrote beneath the floorboards, behind and under drawers. Every time he began a new chapter, he stopped first to calculate how thick would be the resulting manuscript and where best to conceal the bundle of paper.

He knew that, as things stood, no one would publish him. No one could publish him even if they wanted to. A single line of his writing could cost him his life and send a reckless publisher to prison for life. Nevertheless, he continued writing, knowing that this was the only way to remain in possession of his mind.

Whenever he felt that he couldn't stand to conceal his thoughts anymore, that this exaggerated caution wasn't at all his real nature, he admonished himself not to complain. He reminded himself that his life was infinitely better now than in the prison camps. At least, now, he could write on paper. In the forced work camps where no paper was allowed him, he had written everything in his head, committed each word to memory. Although his body had stayed imprisoned in the camp, his memory had slipped the bonds of human limitation. Many times, standing in line for a cup of sickening gruel, he had written sentences in his head, complete with punctuation, rehearsed paragraphs, repeated entire chapters in his head while adding new sections, much like a determined student cramming for an examination.

Yes, now he had paper if not the freedom to publish what he wrote. It was a step in the right direction. He wrote tirelessly, consoling himself with the thought that a person could write good literature without coming face to face with others who possessed more literary experience. He remembered that Tolstoy had once said that the works of a writer should always be published after his death, as a favour to the writer, so he could be left free to write his best without lying. But how not to trouble oneself about publication when one wrote in order to change the here and now? Of what use was publication if it arrived when the present had passed and taken with it the memory and conscience of a people? How to hold one's peace when one was bursting with indignation? How to wait for the right moment? And would the right moment ever come? Would Russia ever open its mind again?

He renewed his vow of anonymity, knowing that any personal contact with any of the known writers would be like reading his latest manuscript at the top of his voice in front of a police station. He consistently obeyed every rule, gave way to every bureaucratic idiocy, gave thanks in the right places and at the right times. Whenever he felt like arguing against some nauseating injustice, he reminded himself that the long haul mattered more; he had already spent eight years in prison, just for criticizing Stalin in a letter to a friend. No, the long haul mattered more now. He was determined not to be arrested again, not until he had produced something worth being arrested for. He continued hiding his manuscripts in unlikely places, haunted by the memory of writers who had paid dearly for the honesty of their talent: Anna Akhmatova, Ivan Bunin, Evgeni Zamyatin, Osip Mandelstam, Varlam Shalamov, Boris Pasternak.

After all he had suffered, it was peculiar that he chose to describe only one day of it. He could have taken the easier path and told his own story just as it had happened, indignation and all. But he told the story of another prisoner. He woke up with him one dawn and stayed with him until the man went to sleep that night. And in that one day, he told the story of an entire generation. Many nights during the writing of the book, as he sat hunched over the thin oilskin paper, his fingers aching from writing the small script, his fury struggled to get the better part of his aesthetic sense. But he reined it in, knowing a writer must rise above his pain and describe the present in the light of a larger reality. With admirable restraint he wrote the story of one innocent bewildered man, falsely denounced and condemned to a forced labour camp. The poor man, whom he gave the fictional name of Ivan Denisovitch, used all his wits to survive, even though he never understood the historical forces that had buried him in an archipelago of abject misery.

*

His young cellmate asks him what crime he has committed.

"It all started with a book I wrote that, miraculously enough, was published in Russia. And then one thing led to another."

"What was the title of the book?" asks the young man.

"*One Day in the Life of Ivan Denisovitch*," he replies.

The young man shakes his head—he hasn't heard of it.

"Then I wrote some other books, *The Inner Circle, Cancer Ward,* and *1914*. And now this one, *The Gulag Archipelago*."

The young man shakes his head again, this time looking a little embarrassed.

"None of my other books were published in Russia. The State confiscated the manuscripts and locked them up. They were published in the West."

"How did the manuscripts get to the West?"

"Some spare copies found their way out of Russia."

The young man nods, impressed. "You mean you wrote things that disturbed them enough to lock you up in this cell?"

"The last book. I'm here because of the last book, *The Gulag Archipelago*. It disturbed them that I refused to leave anything unsaid. They called me a traitor. They said the same thing when I was given the Nobel Prize in 1970. They denounced me for being a pawn in the hands of the West. But what's really driven them crazy is that I refuse to write their version of history."

The young man lets out a slow whistle. "You? The Nobel Prize? You're not pulling my leg, uncle, are you?"

*

The announcement of his nomination for the prize had surprised him. He found it ironic that he was being nominated for books which his own people hadn't been allowed to read.

The State was even more surprised than he was. It reacted furiously to his nomination. It tried everything to discourage the Nobel Committee from choosing him as the winner. It even assembled a high-powered commission of Russian writers to go to Stockholm and denounce the prize. But the announcement that he had won the prize came two weeks earlier than expected. The Nobel Prize for literature was his and there wasn't anything he nor the State could do about it.

He would have liked very much to go in person to receive the prize in Stockholm. But he feared they wouldn't allow him back into Russia. So he wrote a letter to the Nobel committee offering to accept the prize in Moscow. And in his letter he mentioned how he found it ironic that the prize was being presented on the same day as International Human Rights Day. He had a friend deliver the letter to the Swedish embassy and turned back to the half-completed manuscript of *The Gulag Archipelago*.

He stared at the manuscript, trying to remember the sentence he needed to write next. The frequent ringing of the telephone, the fifty or so friends who had been courageous enough to come

by and congratulate him in spite of the KGB agents stationed outside his apartment building ... he had lost track of where he was in
his writing.

The thought came to him with some bitterness: the Nobel
Prize for literature was not for Russian writers. No matter how
good a writer, a controversial Russian winner of the Nobel would
always be accused of being just a pawn in the hands of the West.
Hadn't the awarding of the Nobel Prize in 1933 to Ivan Bunin
elicited the same reaction from the Soviet Establishment? And
hadn't the writer Varlam Shalamov been sentenced that same year
to seventeen years of hard labour in Siberia for uttering the opin-
ion that Ivan Bunin was a great master of Russian literature? And
what about the way the State forced Boris Pasternak to reject the
Nobel Prize in 1958, before viciously persecuting him for allowing *Doctor Zhivago* to be published abroad? No, what mattered to
the State wasn't how well the writer wrote, but what he or she included and what he or she left out.

Come what may he had no intention of leaving anything out in
this latest manuscript. He was determined to tell the story of the
Soviet prison camps, every unbelievable mind-numbing detail,
documented through hundreds of case histories written in a variety of styles: historical, anecdotal, fictional.

He read over the last few paragraphs he had written, chuckling,
knowing that the critics would blame him for letting his own
voice appear in the middle of a narrative section. "There he is giving his troublesome observations. Doesn't he know that literature
should always show and not tell? What's the use of writing a book
that's as much history as fiction? Where's the social realism in
that?" they would say.

But he knew that he was incapable of ignoring the many
themes that presented themselves on the way as he travelled from
the beginning to the middle to the end of a story. There were so
many meanings in a given act. How to talk neatly of one and leave
the rest voiceless without committing a lie of omission against the
mind of the reader?

*

The young man looks puzzled. "Wasn't there a lot of money given for the Nobel Prize? Why didn't you leave then? Why didn't you take the money, say to hell with them, and never come back?"

He tries to explain to the young man that had he done such a thing his work would have amounted to little. Had he left voluntarily the State would not have been forced to reveal its hand to the whole world.

"That's clever," observes the young man. "Didn't Christ say something like that the night before they hung him up on the cross? I would never martyr myself. Not for anything, not even a new Mercedes sports coupe. But fancy that, I'm sharing a cell with a Nobel Prize winner. I hope they're going to mention your imprisonment in the papers. My friends wouldn't believe me unless they saw it printed in the papers."

"Don't worry ... I'm already in the papers," says Solzhenitsyn.

The young man pauses to search his mind and asks in a quieter voice, "You weren't the one were you ... the one they were tarring and feathering in *Pravda*? And the effigy near Gorky Park—"

The young man falls silent, moves over to his cot, lies on it, and thinks for a few minutes. Then he asks, "Uncle ... what is your name again?"

"Alexander Solzhenitsyn."

"Your patronym I mean ... "

"Isayevich."

The young man smiles and shakes his head in amused wonder.

"What are you smiling at?"

"I'm smiling at your name, uncle. Isayevich. It goes back to the prophets. These blokes didn't have a chance with you. I am pleased to know you Alexander Isayevich."

Lying on his cot that night, Solzhenitsyn stares at the light overhead, wondering whether they still require prisoners to sleep with arms placed outside their blankets. He wonders what his wife is doing; whom she has been able to call; if their phone line was left intact after he was taken away; if she managed to take care of the stray papers on his desk; if any of the officers went back to the apartment to search for evidence; if she has received news of his whereabouts; if she herself is safe; if the children are all right.

Next morning. The clanging of metal on the bars of the cells. Then a moment of silence and clanging again. Some hot water, sugar, a gruel, not as sickening as the one served up in the work camps.

They come for him before he's had time to finish the meal and lead him down the hall and into a room. The same prosecutor is presiding; the same watchdogs are seated in a row behind the prisoner's chair.

The prosecutor picks up the document, tunes into the same imperious voice he used the day before, and begins reading:

"By decree of the Presidium of the Supreme ... "

No further words are necessary ... everything is said in those first eight words. The Supreme Soviet has already decided, doesn't need to talk to him about it, isn't interested in asking him for any more information. He could break down and they wouldn't even blink. This is no interrogation. It's the announcement of a decision made long before they went to fetch him at his home.

He listens to the rest of it for the sake of formality. His mind strains for the right response. He won't resist their decision. But he can't leave the country and go into perpetual exile without his wife and children. Anything could happen to them if he leaves the country alone.

He replies, "I will go, but I must take my family with me. They must accompany me."

The prosecutor answers, "They will follow you later."

"What guarantees that they will be allowed to follow?" he asks.

The prosecutor looks at him with amusement, as if surprised that he would worry about such a thing. "They will follow you shortly. We wouldn't dream of keeping you apart," he says ironically.

They escort him back to his cell, hands behind his back. His young cellmate asks him what happened during the interrogation. For a moment he considers telling the young man what was said and decided. But how is he to explain that he is the first man since Trotsky to be stripped of his citizenship and deported from the Soviet Union? How to make him really understand why he didn't leave on his own when he won the money from the Nobel Prize? How to explain that, to make his point, he had to wait until they put him in prison, killed him, or sent him out by force? So he says nothing, deciding it best to let him read it in the papers. Instead, he gives the young man pointers on how to handle an insistent prosecutor when his turns comes for interrogation.

The call to leave the cell. The little cross they took from him is returned. The shoes are outfitted with laces. An officer takes great care to brush the lint off his suit.

And then out into the main hall and into the waiting car. The man sitting next to the driver is the same doctor who examined him in the prison; they aren't taking any chances at all with his chronic high blood pressure.

The car arrives at the airport where a plane has been kept ready, engines humming. They lead him into the plane and point out where he is to sit. There's a fresh crew of KGB men sitting in the aircraft. The doctor sits next to him and offers him special pills to control his high blood pressure. He unwraps the pills from their western packages carefully, as if to reassure him that they aren't poisoned.

Poison. It sets his mind to wondering: what if they are taking him outside the country to kill him? He knows that most Soviet embassies have a secret holding compartment. What if his body is found flung on the side of a highway a few days later?

The plane taxis onto the runway. The doctor asks him if he's feeling all right. Solzhenitsyn nods. As the wheels leave the ground, he looks out the window, crosses himself, and bows to the landscape.

Three hours into the flight. How much longer and where to?

No one has mentioned where he's being taken. He knows better than to expect anything but a blank stare if he asks.

He suspects they're headed for Zurich or Frankfurt. Germany, he recalls, published a promise to receive him if ever he decided to leave Russia. But what if the Germans don't know that he's being flown out of Russia? What will stop his captors from whisking him away to one of their embassy hideouts and finishing him off with complete diplomatic immunity?

He rehearses the landing of the plane ... imagines them escorting him down the gangway, holding his arms the better to bundle him into an unmarked car. He plans how he will call out to the first policeman he sees, repeats in his mind the few phrases of German he knows.

He closes his eyes to avoid the blank stares of the officers on the plane. His mind wanders back to his apartment in Moscow. He sees his desk covered with papers, hundreds of files filled with letters from men and women who sent him their testimonies. He wonders whether it had been worth it to risk his life like that, whether any of it will ever make a difference. But he knows that it would have hurt him more to stay quiet. He had done what he had to do, nothing less and nothing more. What mattered, as much as any future outcome, was that he had done it—proven that one person could remain in possession of his mind by refusing to be part of a lie.

*

And he had refused to be part of the lie throughout the entire three volumes of *The Gulag Archipelago.* Chapter after chapter he had exposed how the regime had been built on a bed of half-truths and outright lies. He had explained how many of the arrests in the thirties were made not because the defendants were truly guilty, but because the state needed manpower to stock its work camps. Why pay people to work when they could be forced to work for ten and a half ounces of bread per day? Russian soldiers who had been taken prisoners of war by the Germans were sent word by Stalin inviting them to return home as heroes. And then they were promptly arrested on their return and, much to their bewilderment, shipped off to prisons and forced work camps.

All the way to the camps the men tried to comprehend what was happening to them. "Why am I here?" and "Why are you here?" they asked each other, over and over again, as they jostled against one another in the cramped railway cars that shuttled them to prison camps buried in the most desolate regions. And even after they were deloused and prisoner identification numbers sewn on their clothing in three different places, they lay on their cots, arms outside their blankets according to camp regulations, and continued to wonder what they had done to deserve such cruel treatment. And then straight to the punishment cells at Sekurnaya Hill they went—wooden poles stretched from wall to wall, placed just high enough so that a prisoner's feet couldn't reach the floor. The prisoner sat there for hours on end like a bird perched in its cage, until finally given the signal and allowed to fall to the floor.

Like a fiend intent on revealing a lie even if it means the collapse of whoever believes in it, he had given precise details, not worrying about the length of the book, knowing that it would be the right length if he told the story without leaving anything out.

He wrote of the camp administrators: how once in awhile, the commander of a camp would pick a few prisoners and liberate them with the announcement that they were innocent. Ingenious, this business of liberating a few after some initial weeks of imprisonment. It implied that those who remained for the next ten, fifteen, or twenty years were being kept behind bars for some good legal reason.

The interrogators were experts at unnerving their prisoners. All an interrogator needed to do to break a courageous man was threaten to arrest his daughter or wife and put her in a cell with syphilitic prisoners. It was at the mention of family that the most stubborn dissenters turned to jelly. They signed whatever was asked of them, gladly confessed to real and imagined transgressions, anything, as long as their tormentors promised to leave their families alone. And those hardy ones who resisted were kept awake night after night, until they fell to their knees and begged to sign whatever paper lay waiting for them. They denounced themselves, their families, their friends, even strangers with whom they had never exchanged a single word, just for a couple of hours of blessed sleep.

He wrote of the strange mix of prisoners in the camps—how they had thrown innocent men in with common murderers and thieves and left them to their mercy. There were two kinds of prisoners in the camps. There were those who really were thieves and murderers, who, under any regime, might be in prison. And then there were those brought in under Article 58 and accused of being Anti Soviet: acting against the State, betraying the motherland, or intending to betray it if only given the chance. For these "58-ers," anything and everything was damning evidence: a word said in anger to the wrong person, silence when there should have been cheering and applause, a book that was read out of curiosity when it should have been turned in to the State unopened, a letter sent to a friend, a page in a diary, failure to meet a given work quota. Many were given ten years for picking up leftover scraps of food at the farm cooperatives. Some were even given ten years for missing a day's work. The entire spectrum of Russian talent was represented in the camps: carpenters, bricklayers, philosophers, historians, plumbers, biologists, blacksmiths, tailors, physicists, poets, novelists, accountants. Each trade had its equal opportunity.

Ten and a half ounces of bread ration per day. Barely enough to keep a person alive. A little more if the prisoner played his cards right and ended up being a trustee, lording it over the other prisoners as an informer or a work foreman. In one section of the Archipelago, they managed to administer thousands of prisoners with only 37 paid guards.

Writing about the nuns and priests he had broken out in tears, set his pen down, and prayed for strength to keep a clear head and write the rest of it. Gritting his teeth, he had described how the camp administrators purposefully locked the priests and nuns in with murderers, prostitutes and thieves, knowing this would devastate them. For good measure, their inquisitors used obscene words while interrogating them, knowing they would be shattered by the vulgarity.

One camp commander developed a favourite way to rid himself of troublesome prisoners. He would have a man tied naked to a post in the yard when the temperature was minus 50 degrees. The shivering man would then be hosed down with ice cold water. The freezing water would cover his body with an icy film, until the layers of ice piled over one another, strangling the man and turning him into an ice sculpture.

Some of the prisoners, witnessing such terrifying scenes, took to pleading their innocence with renewed fervour. But their jailers reminded them that it had never done them any good to try, that they should save themselves the bother and conserve their strength. And strength was all that mattered when a man was on ten and a half ounces of bread a day. If he was determined to survive, he learned to train his body never to make any unnecessary move; instructed his mind to think of nothing except his own survival and regard all others with suspicion

But he hadn't contented himself with merely describing the atrocities. He had gone further and asked his readers to imagine how a warm, generous people had been transformed into a nation which considered trust in a stranger no longer a grace of spirit but a sign of recklessness. How had they managed to tell people, without the slightest bit of sheepishness, that day was night and night was day? The lies and the fear they had spread years ago had hung over Russia like some phantom cloud. The intelligent, independent thinkers had been pushed aside, while the ones who were content to propagate and maintain the lie had been rewarded. And those who spoke out were put away to remind those who stayed silent that they had done well to surrender to their fear and keep their mouths shut.

Describing the people's silent collusion with the regime, he retold the story of one young boy who lost both parents to the prison camps. Left with nowhere to go, he packed a small bag and begged his neighbours to take him in. But they shooed him away and told him to register with the orphanage. He lived in five different orphanages until he was old enough to be on his own. Later, when he was a grown man and his friends asked him about his parents, he shrewdly answered that he didn't know much about them, that they both died in a train accident shortly after he was born.

And then, nearing the end of the book, he had asked the most dangerous question of all. He knew that there would be hell to pay, but he asked it anyway, knowing that it begged to be asked: What about Lenin himself ... wasn't it Lenin who had written, long before Stalin took over the helm, that the party should not hesitate to eliminate anyone who stood in its way? If Lenin had also been behind these purges, then where was the legitimacy of the Party and State which were born in his name?

Making the final revisions to the manuscript, he had wondered what they would do to him if he allowed a Western publisher to bring out the book. He had no illusions. He remembered the writer Bukharin's last words to his wife Anna Larina, when she visited his cell nine hours before his execution: *"I am leaving life. I am lowering my head before a hellish machine, before which I am helpless and which has acquired gigantic power, fabricates organized slander, acts boldly and confidently."*

*

Leaning back in his seat, he surveys the expressionless faces of the KGB agents accompanying him on this flight. He wonders what their lives might have been had he and they lived in a free nation. He might have written stories just for the sake of telling them. He might even have felt proud to write about them, glad to have them standing next to him as free people, capable of disagreeing with him and even rebelling against the plots he imagined for them. But it had been a peculiar time and he had been there in the midst of it and no imagined plots had been needed. He had done what the artist in him had needed to do—describe what he had seen without apologizing for it or leaving any of it out. Some in Russia and the West had accused him of sounding like a cantankerous prophet in the wilderness. He would have preferred them to mention that there really had been a wilderness, a wilderness that might have turned into something far more terrible had no one howled in protest.

*

He comes out of his reverie and looks at his watch, realizing with deep sadness that Russia is far away and his place of exile nearing by the minute. The officers sitting opposite him stare at him stonily. He gets up to go to the toilet. They hurry after him and don't permit him to close the door. Leading him back to his seat, they offer him sweets, biscuits and coffee.

Every so often the doctor asks him whether he's feeling all right. The poor man knows what the State will do to him if the prisoner dies on the way and unleashes an international scandal.

The plane lands on the runway. A sign rushes past: "Frankfurt am Main." The doctor lets out a sigh of relief. The plane taxis in front of a building and comes to a stop. They tell him to stand up and leave the plane. It's nearly five o'clock, twenty-four hours since they arrived at his apartment promising they'd have him back in two hours.

He steps through the doorway and starts down the gangway. A few steps down, he turns to look see which of them are accompanying him. But there's no one. He's on his own. This time they really want to be done with him.

A couple of hundred people are gathered on the tarmac. There are flashing bulbs, video cameras, flood lights, enthusiastic applause. As he reaches the bottom of the gangway, a man steps forward and introduces himself as a representative of the Ministry of Foreign Affairs of the Federal Republic of Germany. A well-dressed woman presents him with a bouquet of flowers. A number of reporters crowd in, asking for a statement. Now that he's free, he can say anything he wants, no one will punish him. What would he like to say?

Looking around the reporters with their expectant faces, their microphones waving crazily, he finds his mind returning to Russia. He thinks of his books, the thousands of pages of manuscript written as witness to his country's suffering. What can he say that will not betray this testament? Slowly the corners of his mouth turn down—then lifting his head so that he is staring directly into the flashing lights, he responds gently but firmly: "I will be remaining silent for now."

October 30th

The TV anchorman turns to the anchorwoman working with him and says, "The YES is leading by one-and-a-half percent." Then, he locks eyes with the camera and says, "We expect this to shape up into a very long evening. No one can call this one just yet. Sit back. This is going to be longer than 1980." The anchorwoman nods her head and smiles, just enough to acknowledge the excitement of the situation but not enough to discount its gravity.

Figures flash on the screen. On each side of the screen are the designations of the vote: YES and NO. Under each designation is a bar that grows or shrinks according to the latest reports. The YES bar is blue, in keeping with the blue in the flag of Quebec. The NO bar is red, in keeping with the colour of the Canadian flag.

"We've just had some more polling stations coming in. The lead of the YES forces is down by half a percentage point." The YES bar shrinks a little to make way for the expanding NO bar. The bars have been set up to move back and forth without separating from one another. Any movement on one side triggers an opposite movement on the other, like a tug-of-war game with a kerchief tied at midpoint.

The anchorwoman turns to interview a financial analyst. She asks the analyst what he thinks will happen to the Canadian dollar if Quebec votes to separate. The analyst blinks rapidly. He replies that the markets have quieted down for the day, but that investors are standing by on the fringes, waiting for the final result before making their next move. The anchorwoman presses on. She wants to know what will happen to the Canadian dollar if the YES side wins. The analyst tilts his head to one side, raises his eyebrows, and says in a level voice that the dollar could lose fifteen to twenty percent of its value.

Nabil checks his watch. He gets up from the couch, walks into the kitchen, opens the fridge, and takes out a pot. He slides the pot into the oven and sets the timer.

The telephone rings just as he is about to walk back to the television set.

"*Merhaba*, Nabil. So did you vote?" asks his friend Murad.

"*Merhaba*, Murad. Yes, I voted this morning," answers Nabil.

"What do you think is going to happen?" asks Murad.

"I don't know. Nobody knows," says Nabil.

"Pray that if the YES side loses, that it loses big."

"Why?" asks Nabil.

"Everyone knows the ethnic minorities are against separation in a heavy way. If the separatists lose by a small margin, they'll blame their losing on us. That's why, *habibi*."

"It's a democratic place. We're not in Lebanon anymore."

"Yeah? The whole world is Lebanon. Bosnia is Lebanon. Somalia was Lebanon—"

"This isn't Lebanon," repeats Nabil.

"Chechnya is Lebanon. Moscow is Lebanon. The whole goddamned world is Lebanon. The human heart is Lebanon. Lebanon is Lebanon, even though it doesn't want to admit it."

"People do things differently here," prompts Nabil.

"That won't stop them from blaming us. You'll see the looks they give us if they lose by a narrow margin. Get ready to become an invisible minority if they win," says Murad.

"I've never had trouble here. Anyway, if the NO side wins, the francophones who voted NO will appreciate your support. It'll balance things out."

"Don't count on it. They'll shake our hands and thank us. But will they give you a job in their bureaucracy? Will they ask you home to meet their daughters? No, nothing will balance things out after this. There will always be something."

"Why do you always talk in terms of *them and us*?"

"Allah! Because they themselves talk in terms of *them and us*. That's why. Once in my political science class we were talking of Quebec and I said *we*. A couple of them stared at me. Politely, of course, but they *did* stare."

"It'll be settled in a couple of hours," says Nabil, glancing at his watch.

"I'm telling you, it's going to be a mess," presses Murad.

"It'll be all right," says Nabil.

"It'll never be all right after tonight."

"Relax, *habibi*. This isn't Beirut. Relax."

"I told you, the whole world is Beirut."

"I've got to get dinner ready. Giselle's arriving—"

"Thank God you're living with someone who's voting NO. Imagine what hell you would be in if she was voting YES. She would try to talk you into voting YES too. What a mess it would be. Thank God she's voting NO."

"It's a free country," says Nabil.

"Maybe the country is free. But people are people. Anyway, I'm glad we're on the same side. Imagine you a Christian from Beirut, and me a Muslim from Beirut, and we're on the same side for a change."

Nabil remains silent and glances at the timer on the oven.

Murad says, "I'll call you later tonight and we'll celebrate. Say hello to Giselle. Ya-allah, goodbye. I'm going back to the TV set."

Nabil hangs up the phone and walks into the living room. He stands in front of the TV and stares at the screen.

The NO bar reads 48.23 percent, the YES bar 51.77 percent. There's a box on the screen indicating the numbers of electoral districts that have reported their results. The anchorman shakes his head in wonder. He says that this is a real teeth-grinder. He turns to a political analyst and asks her what changes the federal government might propose should the NO side win. She says a few reassuring words and then there's a film clip of a premier from a western province affirming that Quebec is loved, that everything will be done to give Quebec the final decision on its own culture. The premier adds that his own province would like to see the federal government decentralize, for the benefit of all the provinces.

There is the sound of a key turning in the front door. Nabil walks back into the kitchen and waits by the oven. He wipes the sweat off his palms. Giselle comes into the kitchen. "It's good to be home," she says. "You should have seen the polling station. C'était très, très occupé. I waited in line for nearly an hour."

Giselle hugs Nabil. They embrace for a further moment and then she says, "It felt strange. We were all looking at one another at the polling station, not knowing which of us was voting which way. Everyone looked very reserved. It was tense. I'm glad I'm home."

Giselle tightens her arms around Nabil's neck and kisses him. "Yumm ... what's in there?" she asks, glancing at the oven.

"Lasagna," answers Nabil. "We can eat dinner and then watch the results on TV. They say it's going to be a long night."

Nabil opens the door of the oven and slips out the casserole. Giselle sits at the kitchen table, pours herself a glass of wine, then falls silent and stares into her glass.

"What's wrong?" asks Nabil, bringing the casserole over to the table.

"I'm very worried. You should have seen everyone at work today. It was tense. The owner of the plant sent every one of us a memo saying that if the YES side won, he would move the plant to Ontario, maybe even to the States. There were a couple of separatists who were really insulted by the memo. They complained to the union rep that he was strong-arming them to vote NO. The owner said it was only a matter of economics. And there's a Filipino who works next to my station. The poor man was on the verge of tears. He asked me if he could prove to the owner that he would vote NO."

"What did you say?"

"I explained to him that the ballot is secret, that nobody sees what you vote. That it's a democracy. Imagine, he asked if he could ask for a photocopy of his ballot before he threw it in the box. The poor man was terrified the plant would move. I'm worried too. This thing is too close. Do you realize that this could be the last dinner we have in Canada? It's ridiculous! C'est vraiment stupide! This could be our last dinner as Canadians!"

Nabil sits down at the table and serves the meal.

"What are we going to do if Quebec separates? What's going to happen to the economy? What about our passports? I can't believe it that people are voting YES to separation without thinking of all these horrible details."

"Maybe they are thinking," offers Nabil.

"No, they're not. They said it on the news. A lot of people still think that they will be sending representatives to the Canadian parliament even after they separate. I mean where are these people coming from? How can they not understand what they're voting for? Ça m'énerve!"

"Maybe it's because there was a lot of talk of cooperation and partnership if they separate. Anyway, what's said depends on which channel you're watching," says Nabil.

Giselle gets up from the table and walks over to the television set. She stands in front of the set, chin cupped in hand. The anchorman is shaking his head, "If you've just tuned in, this referendum is really unbelievable! You can cut the tension in Quebec. It can't get tighter than this! The vote is very very close."

Giselle shouts to Nabil from the living room. "Did you hear that? It's almost a dead heat. Oh, mon Dieu, je suis soulagé. There's still hope. And the Montreal vote is just starting to come in. There's still a good chance. Can you imagine what would happen if the final result was fifty-fifty, with the exact same number of votes on each side?"

"Someone would probably say it was a sign from God. Come and eat. We'll watch later. It's going to take a long time for this thing. Come eat your lasagna."

Giselle returns to the table and resumes eating. She smiles tenderly. "I was thinking yesterday ... it's four years and we're still together."

"Your mother thought I'd be too macho for you," says Nabil. They both giggle. Giselle reaches across the table and caresses Nabil's face.

"Nabil, pray this thing blows over. I'm scared. Pray that the NO wins, that it's over and we can go to bed tonight, hold each other and be happy."

"They want their own country," says Nabil softly.

"Well they're not going to have it. I'm Québecoise, pure laine, as the premier would put it, but I say they won't have their lunatic wish. We're in a globalized world now. It's too late for this nonsense. They've been going on about this for decades. I've been hearing it ever since I was a kid. I'm tired of it."

"I think some of them really want to feel like citizens of their own country," says Nabil. "They speak a different language and they live differently. They want a country to go with it. Maybe this is more than just contradicting the rest of Canada." He lays his fork down and fiddles with the napkin resting next to his plate. Giselle puts her fork down too and looks into Nabil's face. He pulls his eyes away and goes back to eating.

"C'est idiot! I don't want a new country. I already have a country. It's called Canada. It's not perfect, but it's good enough for me. C'est NON, NON, NON. Pray we win—it won't be funny if the OUI comes in! We are a people and that's enough for me. But no country business! Pas de pays."

"Some want their own country," repeats Nabil.

Giselle puts a forkful of food back down on her plate. "Veux tu arrêter! What country are you talking about? Who are we going to trade with? What about the money? The passports? Your problem is you're always trying to be objective. It's a good part of you. Normally I like it. But not tonight. Tonight, there's only one way—and that is NO."

"Still … I think I understand some of them," says Nabil, staring into his plate.

Giselle gets up brusquely. She turns away from Nabil and walks over to the television. "Damn it, they're still ahead!" says Giselle.

"What's the damned use if they have only a half a percent lead? Veux tu me le dire? Ey? The federal government will never accept it. Ottawa will say it's not enough of a majority. The whole thing is useless. I don't know why they don't just give up right now."

"The voting is over. It's done. They can't give up," says Nabil. He gets up from his chair and walks into the living room. He puts his arms around Giselle and they fall back onto the couch.

"If Montreal is the only city that votes NO by a large majority it's not going to be funny for the foreigners. Murad says the ethnic communities will be blamed."

Giselle shakes her head, "Nonsense. Non, non. Quebec isn't like that. We're a democracy. Every vote counts, no matter whose it is."

"I don't know. I wonder. I mean, after all, say your grandfather and father wanted a country and now you wanted a country—"

"I don't."

"But say you did and a lot of other francophones wanted a country of their own too and the majority of you voted for it but then you lost the vote because the non-Francophones voted against it in a big way. It might be hard to stay objective. Wouldn't it leave a bitter taste in your mouth?"

"My mouth won't be bitter at all—not if we win," answers Giselle. "It will be very sweet. Très douce." She turns to Nabil and gives him a long kiss.

The anchor announces that seventy-five percent of the regions have reported. Nabil reaches over to the coffee table and picks up the remote control. He switches over to the French channel. The headquarters of the YES side is on screen. Supporters are chanting and waving the flags of Quebec. An on-location reporter comes on screen and announces that the mood in the YES camp is "Optimistic."

"Optimism?" shouts Giselle. "I want to see your optimism six months from now if you win. We'll all be starving. We'll all be eating 99-cent macaroni." She grabs the remote control and switches back to the English channel.

"Money isn't everything," says Nabil, holding Giselle a little tighter.

Giselle pulls away from Nabil's arms. "Why are you rationalizing for them?" she asks.

Nabil stays silent. He tries pulling her back to him, but she pulls away. "Non, non, wow, minute—tell me, why are you so ready to speak on their behalf? You're trying to make them look like saints."

"I'm just trying to show you how some of them may feel. I mean they're your own people. But you don't seem to have much sympathy for how they feel."

"I have no more patience left for them. They're not my kind of people. I'm not tribal." She pauses and adds, "And since when did it become your business to make me feel for my own people?"

"You mean I should stay out of it because I'm not a francophone?"

"Non, idiot. Don't get touchy. I mean you and I are both NO. We don't need to argue about these stupidities. Another hour and it'll be over. We'll be in bed making love. Our lives will go on."

"Why don't I have a right to feel for them?" presses Nabil.

"Oh, mon Dieu. Veux tu arrêter! Fine, go feel all you want. Go to church if you want and pray for them. Light a dozen candles. Wail for them. Moi, je suis bien. I don't want to have anything to do with their sovereignty."

Nabil says, hesitantly, "Maybe it feels nice ... I mean to have your own country. Look at the English in the other provinces—they're English and they feel they have their own country. So they consider Quebec an equal partner and consider it a member of their group. But maybe it feels good not to be just a district or province or member with a strange language. You know, like to be all together, your own group, like a body with its own arms and legs—"

"Yeah, emaciated arms and legs if the YES wins," says Giselle.

"Nobody knows the future," says Nabil.

Giselle turns away from the screen and glares at him. "You're really doing your best to get on my nerves tonight, ey? It's not enough that the whole city is hyperventilating?"

"I remember when Beirut split apart. I was a small boy then. During the war we took to playing with toy guns instead of toy trucks. We would form two groups and pretend we were all commandos. The merchants made a lot of money selling us toy guns."

"So you've seen what happens. You know separation is bad. Why do you talk this nonsense and try to make it sound sane?"

"Beirut never became the same again," continues Nabil. "My cousin Fouad stayed there. He still writes me that everywhere you look you see bullet holes, as if the architects put them there as decorative touches."

The TV anchor announces that some more electoral districts are beginning to report from Montreal. The vote is still in favour of the YES. There are some beads of perspiration on the anchor's forehead. Nabil switches the TV to the French channel.

"Don't change it. Leave it on the CBC," snaps Giselle.

"Just a minute," says Nabil, concentrating on the screen. The French channel is broadcasting from the headquarters of the YES side. The flags aren't being waved any longer. Thousands of YES supporters are staring silently at the giant monitors.

"Mais, oui! Now they look worried. Now they come to their senses," says Giselle.

Nabil stares at the screen intently. Some of the people on camera have tears running down their faces.

Giselle continues, "Where's their confidence now? They threw the whole country into chaos and now they're silent. Allez-y, pleurer!"

Nabil stays silent. Giselle turns from the screen and glances at him.

"You look too damned serious. You know we're going to win. What's the problem?"

"Well, it is serious. I don't think any side is really going to win. This isn't the end of it," says Nabil, keeping his eyes on the screen.

"Yes it is. We're winning. There won't be any referendums after this one." Then, an afterthought, "What time did you vote today?"

"I went this morning, on the way to work."

"Was it very crowded?"

"Yes. I got caught in the morning rush hour vote."

"Did you take Murad with you?"

"No ... I went alone."

"You said you two were going together. Weren't you supposed to give him a ride?"

"I asked him to take the bus. I went alone."

"Why?"

"I wanted to be alone."

"What for?"

"To think."

Giselle's voice rises slightly. "Think? Think about what?"

"Everything. Here. Lebanon. Canada. Everywhere. I was thinking about what would have happened if we hadn't had a war in Beirut."

"You're in Quebec now. What does Beirut have to do with it? Leave Beirut to solve its own problems."

"I mean when I lived there it was my country. I was raised there, played in its streets, saw its flag on street corners. But when I emigrated here, I didn't have a country anymore. I was Lebanese ... Lebanese-Canadian-Québecois. I don't know what. Mixed up, like a tabouleh."

"Are you telling me you're homesick?"

"No. I don't have a country anymore. Not Lebanon, not after fifteen years. How can I be homesick without a home?"

"You have Canada."

"No, Canada feels too far. It feels like on the other side of the Quebec border, in some other town."

"Then pretend Quebec is your home. It's right under your feet ... as long as you vote NO."

"This morning I was thinking it would be nice to have a country, something close-by that surrounds you and comforts you."

Giselle's eyes widen. The anchorman announces that the NO side has edged forward and is leading by a third of a percentage point.

"What the hell are you talking about, Nabil?" asks Giselle, straightening her back.

"I started ... " Nabil hesitates, then continues, looking into Giselle's eyes pleadingly. "I ... started feeling what they were feeling and ... I don't know. I got to the ballot box and I voted YES. It just happened."

Giselle stares at him. Her mouth falls open. Nabil lowers his eyes and switches the remote back to the English station. The NO headquarters is on screen now. The crowd is waving Canadian and Quebec flags. Hundreds of people are waving at the camera, chanting "Canada! Canada!"

Giselle gets up from the couch. Nabil reaches forward to take her by the hand. She jerks it away. "Don't touch me!" she snaps.

Nabil pleads, "Don't be like that. I told you. It's been a long time since I have felt like this. We used to be very patriotic in Lebanon. I miss that. Canada is too neutral, too spread out. I wanted something that was together—"

"I don't believe this," hisses Giselle. She stomps into the kitchen and pours herself a glass of wine. She comes back into the living room and puts her shoes on. "Tell me you were joking. This is no time for jokes. Tell me you're joking."

"No, I mean it. J'ai voté OUI."

Giselle swallows the wine in one long gulp. She glares at Nabil, then hurls the glass at the wall. "Maudit! You voted OUI?"

She disappears into the bedroom and comes out with an empty suitcase.

"What's that for?" asks Nabil. For a moment his heart takes to skipping wildly. "It's no big deal. The NO is winning. So it makes no difference anymore," he says.

"No big deal? You betrayed us. You betrayed me. No big deal! You and I were NO. You broke away and went over to the OUI. There's the suitcase. If you don't like it here in Canada, you can leave. But don't start sticking your nose in affairs you know nothing about."

"I didn't break away. I just followed a feeling," he says.

"You don't understand what's involved here. You could never have voted YES if you did. You couldn't have betrayed us like you did." She clutches one of the couch pillows, folds herself around it. "You don't understand. You betrayed us."

"I've lived here for fifteen years. I've seen a lot. I understand more than you think. I'm not a traitor."

"Your brain is still in Beirut. You're still shellshocked. Go visit the dead-broke villages in Gaspésie before being so optimistic."

"My brain isn't in Beirut. My brain is right here and I've seen the dead-broke. I drove through Quebec one summer. I saw a lot. I just wanted a country of my own. I voted for me ... and maybe for them too."

"Then you can all go build your country up in the Yukon and wait for the Americans to arrive."

"I don't believe what you're saying. That's what the English have been saying to the French all these years. Shut up and put up with it or be swallowed whole by the Americans."

"Yes, that's what I said. And a lot of others are saying it too. Shut up and put up with it, or go back to your own bullet museum country. And while you're at it, take the whole YES camp with you. Give them a taste of what it's like to live in a broken country."

"Lebanon wasn't broken. It was shattered. Why are we arguing, anyway? This is silly."

Giselle gets up and stomps to her own separate armchair, cutting through the air with clenched fists. "Unbelievable! I've lived with you for four years and I haven't known you. Tell me. What else don't I know? What else have you kept hidden? Mistresses? Separate bank accounts? What else don't I know?"

"For God's sake. I'm the same person. I just voted YES. I just decided it this morning when I got to the voting station. I love you just the same."

"Just decided this morning? I don't believe you decided this morning. All this time you've been telling me you're on the NO side. Just to keep me asleep. Jésus! I don't believe you went and voted to break up this country that received you so generously."

"Generously—?"

"Yes, generously! As a refugee! You betrayed this country's generosity."

"They also received rich business people who each brought in at least a quarter of a million dollars cash. So what difference does it make?"

"A world of difference! You agreed to be loyal when you took the Canadian citizenship oath. You broke that oath today."

"You don't understand. It's a pity, because I care about this place, this whole place, Canada and Quebec and everywhere else. It's sad that you don't understand."

"If you cared, you would have left well enough alone. We have recognition—our language, our culture, our singers, our films, our educational system. What else do they want?"

"I don't know," answers Nabil in a quiet voice. "They must be missing something. Maybe they want to be recognized as a people, different from the rest. Not just because of language. Like a different people. Maybe they want someone to recognize their pain."

"Pain? You're crazy. You make me sick."

"You're abusing me."

"You abused the entire province."

"This isn't getting anywhere," says Nabil, shaking his head sadly.

"Maybe it is. Maybe it's showing us that we made a mistake with each other," says Giselle.

"What mistake?"

"Living together. Maybe we jumped into it too quickly."

"But it's been four years. We've been good for each other."

"Yeah good. As long as I pretended you understood me. And as long as you pretended you were something that you weren't."

"I do understand you. You voted NO because you're worried, because you believe in what you do. It's okay."

"Non, non. More than that. Because I am proud to be a Canadian."

"I'm proud too."

"You can't be having supper at the houses of two different aunts in the same evening. You made your choice without even telling me."

"You would have exploded if I had said anything. In any case, it happened only this morning."

"Yes, I would have been sick to my stomach if you had told me, just as I am now. But now it's even worse. It's like something terrible has been done behind my back."

"Giselle, écoute … il faut qu'on arrête. This is stupid."

"Maybe we made a big mistake. Maybe, my mother was right."

"Your mother—"

"Nothing, forget it."

"No, I want to know. Right about what?"

Giselle hesitates, but continues. "About me being French and you from a foreign place. She told me that we'd never see eye to eye. Maybe she knew what she was talking about. Maybe your people and my people are different."

Nabil stays silent.

"Nabil … "

"Yes … "

"Nabil … I can't … I think it's better you take your things now."

"Where? Why? Don't be crazy."

"It's not going to work. Just please, let's not make things worse. Just take your things and maybe later we can be friends someday."

"You mean you want us to break up over a ballot?"

"Not over a ballot. Over a country. A beautiful country. The number one country in the world."

Nabil gets up from the couch and walks to the edge of the room, slowly, like a sleepwalker. He turns to look at Giselle. She turns her face away and stares at the TV screen. The anchorman announces jubilantly that 90 percent of the vote is in and the NO side is winning by a margin of nearly one percent. Nabil picks up the empty suitcase and walks into the bedroom.

Giselle switches the channel to a scene of the YES headquarters. The premier is pacing the floor, realizing that the campaign is nearly lost. She wonders how many prepared speeches he has in his jacket pocket. The screen transfers to the NO headquarters. There's pandemonium. Flags waving, people hugging, faces painted with the red maple leaf. The anchor reports, "Not a large win. But the jubilation is there nonetheless. A majority of Quebecers, by a slim margin, have voted to stay with Canada. The Premier of Quebec will be addressing the crowd soon and we'll have a broadcast from the office of the Prime Minister of Canada shortly after. This has been a very long nerve-wracking evening."

Giselle shuts her eyes. She massages her pounding temples. Nabil comes out of the bedroom carrying the suitcase. He walks to the front door, then hesitates, hoping she will stop him from leaving. When Giselle continues staring at the TV screen, he walks out the door and shuts it behind him.

A moment later, the Premier of Quebec takes the podium. As he starts speaking, Giselle screams at him, "Maudit imbécile! You ruined the man I loved!"

The Premier begins reading from his speech. He says that the vote was very close, that 60 percent of real French-Canadians voted YES. That they lost only because of money interests and the ethnic vote. At these words, the camera quickly pans the faces in the crowd. Many in the audience cringe at his comments. A few applaud. Giselle starts laughing hysterically. She switches the TV off and bursts into tears.

*

Nabil is out of the apartment building and in the street. "We want our country!" chant a group of disappointed YES supporters who are walking up the block. They're carrying the flag of Quebec. As they pass by, one of the young men in the group looks at Nabil with suspicion. Another stops and asks him in English, "Did you vote NO or YES?" Nabil thinks about what to reply. "I didn't vote," he lies. "I didn't feel I should interfere." The young man pats him on the shoulder and says, "Maybe next time, mon ami, you will vote YES and interfere in our favour?" Nabil answers, "Yes, next time." The young man gives Nabil another

friendly pat on the shoulder and joins his friends. They continue
walking down the street waving the flag and chanting "Vive le
Québec libre!"

Nabil looks back at the house and sees Giselle's silhouette at the
window. He walks down the street and turns onto the main road
wandering towards the centre of town, not certain of his destina-
tion, his mind reeling with the sounds of the helicopters hovering
over the city. Once in a while, honking cars pass him, their occu-
pants waving flags, alternately chanting "Quebec!" — "Canada!"

He arrives at a café and decides to have a coffee to steady his
nerves. The café is empty except for the man behind the counter.
It's just past three in the morning. "C'est ouvert?" Nabil asks.

The man glances at him and turns his back. Nabil asks again,
thinking the man hasn't heard. The man answers, "The doors are
open. See for yourself. I don't have time for stupid talk."

"Is something making you angry?"

The man moves further down the counter, back still turned on
Nabil, and mutters, "Yes, something is making me angry."

"Would it have anything to do with the results?"

"Yes, it would," growls the man, turning just enough to throw
Nabil a sharp accusatory look.

"Leave me out of it, please," says Nabil. "In fact, my girlfriend
who voted NO threw me out of our apartment because I voted
YES. So I wish I hadn't even voted. Please don't be ridiculous.
We're both people. I know how you feel. But please don't be
ridiculous." The man at the counter turns to Nabil, gives him the
finger, then ceremoniously turns his back on Nabil, bends forward
and farts.

Nabil falls silent. Then, recovering, he says, "This is not right. I
can make a civil complaint against you."

The man answers, "Get out or I'll give you a real reason to make
a complaint."

Nabil walks out of the café, ruminating on the bitter irony of
the evening's events. He finds his way to the central train station
and walks into the nearly deserted terminal. He sits on a bench

and wipes the sweat off his forehead. He remembers arriving at this same terminal years ago, glad to be beginning a new life, re- members sitting on one of these same benches. He hadn't known English then, only Arabic and French. He takes a deep breath to push down the tears and shuts his tired eyes.

A policeman patrolling the station walks over to him and asks him if he's waiting to take a train. Nabil pauses and then explains what has just happened to him in the café.

The policeman is incensed. "Moi, j'ai voté NO," he says. "That fellow who insulted you is a loser ... go take your train, sir, and leave him in our hands. We'll set him straight. You just point out the café. I'll see to it."

"No, don't bother him. I just needed to tell someone. Leave the man alone."

The policeman shakes his head, "These things can't be allowed. The man needs speaking to. We can't have this in Quebec." Then giving Nabil a warm smile, he adds, "I'm glad you voted NO. We have to keep this place together ... all of us have to."

Nabil remembers Giselle's furious face and the café operator's glance of smouldering hatred. "I didn't vote. I'm not a citizen yet," he lies.

"Well, I hope that when you do become a citizen, you con- sider this very carefully and vote NO. We need the votes of every- one. Don't be seduced by all this talk of patrimony. NON c'est NON!"

Nabil thanks the police officer, asks again that the café operator be left alone, and moves to another bench. He remembers a year ago when he brought an old friend to the train station to see him off to Toronto. His friend's last words to him were, "It's no use. I'll never feel wanted here. I'm never coming back here."

He leans his head back and wipes his eyes on his sleeve. Then more tears, as his mind travels to the rubble-torn neighbourhood in Beirut, the shattered remains of his father's house, the kids play- ing in the streets with toy guns made of carved wood.

The station master's voice comes on the public address system.

He announces that the train for Toronto is leaving in five minutes. He announces it in French and in English, just as has been done for decades.

Nabil gets up wearily and walks over to a phone booth. He sets down his suitcase and stands there for a long while. Then he dips into his pocket, takes out a coin, and dials the number of the apartment he and Giselle have shared for the past four years.

"Where are you?" answers Giselle sleepily.

"The train station."

"What are you doing there? Where are you going?" asks Giselle, a sudden worry in her voice.

"Nowhere. The whole world is Lebanon. Everywhere is everywhere else. So why go anywhere?"

"Stop babbling and come home. I miss you."

"Come home?" echoes Nabil, staring at the passengers lined up for the Toronto express. "Yes," he adds slowly, "it would be good to come home."

About the Author

Benet Davetian is a Canadian writer based in Montreal. His fiction draws on a wealth of experience gained while living and travelling in Western and Eastern Europe, Africa, the Middle East, Asia and the United States.

He is the author of the best-selling *The Montreal Experience* and *Reprieve in Sarajevo*. His short stories and essays on culture and literature have appeared in Canadian and American reviews. He is the recipient of various communications awards and fellowships, including the Telegram "Care" award for creative achievement. Among his current projects are two novels, *Diary of an Unknown Man* and *Dialogues in the Dark*.